How to Fly with Broken Wings

JANE ELSON

Hodder
Children's
Books

HODDER CHILDREN'S BOOKS

First published in Great Britain in 2015 by Hodder and Stoughton

7 9 10 8

A CIP catalogue record for this book
is available from the British Library.

ISBN 978 1 444 91676 8

Typeset in Egyptian 505 BT and DIN Light by Avon DataSet Ltd,
Bidford-on-Avon, Warwickshire

Printed and bound in Great Britain by Clays Ltd, Elcograf S.p.A.

The paper and board used in this book are made from wood
from responsible sources.

Hodder Children's Books
An imprint of Hachette Children's Group
Part of Hodder and Stoughton
Carmelite House
50 Victoria Embankment
London EC4Y 0DZ

An Hachette UK Company
www.hachette.co.uk

www.hachettechildrens.co.uk

For Clare who played on the beach in Norfolk as a child while the Spitfires swarmed overhead like bees.

'The moment you doubt whether you can fly,
you cease forever to be able to do it.'

J M Barrie, *Peter Pan*

This is my poem I wrote in English. I got 3 merit marks for it.

Gran has stuck it on the fridge with her *A Gift from Bournemouth* magnet.

Sounds in my Head
by Willem Edward Smith

At day time
I open my window.
I hear the birds sing and the flap of their wings inside my head.
Those are good sounds.
If there are people near me and shouting and phones ringing and cars
roaring and hoovers and hairdryers – and – and – and – all the bad sounds
My world melts.
At night-time
If there are no sounds to you the silence crackles to me.

I, Willem Edward Smith, know that you need an aeroplane or wings to fly.

That is a fact.

Dreams know no facts.

At night-time my arms become wings and I fly up, up, up, into the sky.

This first happened 4 years ago on the night when I was 8 years, 2 months and 3 days.

Sometimes I fly in the day as well. I count to 10 and up I go into the clouds.

This is called a daydream.

It is my secret.

This is the story of the day I let my secret out.

1

WILLEM

When Finn Mason shouts 'jump', you jump as high as you can or you are dead.

I took a deep breath.

'Jump, you muppet,' yelled Finn, a dot of spit escaping from the corner of his mouth.

TJ and Laurence stood either side of him. They were staring up at me. Their mouths were open.

I inched my toes forward over the edge of the school wall. A bit of the broken glass that Mr Patricks, our school caretaker, had spread along the top to keep us *in* school and burglars *out* of school, scrunched under my feet. No burglars would ever want to come into our school because there is nothing left to steal. Finn Mason has stolen everything already.

'Jump! Jump! Jump!' chanted Laurence and TJ. Laurence was laughing. TJ looked as if he was about to be sick. My fingers started to jiggle.

I reached into my right pocket for my model of a Spitfire Mark 1.

It had gone! Spinning the propeller calms my hands and helps me focus on solving difficult problems, for example this one where I am being forced to jump off a very high wall. I pushed my hand into my left pocket even though it is a fact that I always keep my model Spitfire Mark 1 in my right pocket. It was not there. It was lost. My fingers jiggled faster.

I should not have been on top of the school wall. I should have been doing my homework. Mrs Hubert, my Maths teacher had given me different homework from the rest of the class. They had to complete 10 equations.

I had to make 2 friends.

Mrs Hubert said that my gran does not count because she is a relative. Bernie from Bernie's Burger Bar does not count because he is a shopkeeper. I asked Mrs Hubert if she was my friend and she said no, she is my Maths teacher.

'You must make 2 friends your own age,' she said.

'Jump!' screamed Finn.

He is not my friend.

I inched a bit further forward.

A piece of glass went through the thin bit at the bottom of my left, black, second-favourite school lace-ups and cut into my big toe.

Mr Patricks should not put glass on top of the wall because of health and safety. Mr Patricks should not be a school caretaker. He should be an SAS assassin.

It's funny, isn't it, the things that go through your mind when you are about to jump off a wall and die?

An aeroplane droned above me. I looked up. I think it was a Boeing 747-400, but it is hard to tell when you are trying to balance on top of a very high wall. They can fly without stopping for up to 7,670 nautical miles. Aeroplane facts make me feel calm.

'Jump,' shouted Finn.

Finn has blond curls on his head. He does not comb his hair. He has 7 freckles on his nose. I counted them when he made me jump off my school desk yesterday at breaktime. Finn, TJ and Laurence looked very small from up on the wall.

'I said JUMP!' screamed Finn.

I looked down.

I, Willem Edward Smith, would like to state here to you that I am not afraid of heights. We live on the 18th floor of the Beckham Estate. 'We sleep higher than the birds,' says my gran. If I was about to die then I was going to ask whoever is in charge up there – say God or, if I couldn't get to see him, his assistant St Peter – if I could come back as a bird because I do not like being Willem Edward Smith very much.

My Gran says to *always go to the top*. So I hoped God was available for my request. Maybe I could make an appointment with him.

Another thing my Gran says is that *I must plan for everything* so that I don't get any nasty surprises in life. So whenever I see Finn walking down the school corridor I always start jumping up and down on the spot before he can tell me to. I ruffle my hair and pull a button off my shirt and smack myself in the face so I have a red mark on my cheek. My plan is that Finn will think he has beaten me up already.

Finn has a short attention span so sometimes this works, but other times he makes me jump higher and kicks me in the stomach.

'Jump! Jump! Jump!' they chanted louder and louder.

My fingers jiggled faster. Who would make Gran her morning cup of tea and bring her a plate of digestive biscuits if I died jumping off the school wall? Which, by the way, I thought would be a pitiful way to end my very short life of 12 years and I started to count the days, minutes and seconds I had been on Planet Earth.

'Jump, you pathetic piece of filth.' Finn interrupted my calculation.

I took another deep breath and inched my toes further over the edge. The ground started to spin. I wobbled. TJ put his hands over his eyes. A girl screamed.

Sasha Barton was running towards us.

'Finn, what are you doing? If you hurt him you'll be chucked out of school again and we won't see each other. Not ever. My dad will ban you from my life for the sixth time this year.'

Sasha looked up at me and did the tiniest of

winks. It was barely a flicker, but I saw it. If someone winks at you, does that mean that they are your friend? Then she flicked her long black hair behind her ears, shook her gold hoop earrings and flung her arms around Finn.

'Leave Willem alone, Finn, *please*,' she said, staring into his eyes.

Finn did not look into Sasha's eyes. He stared at her bumps. Except her bumps are not very big – not big enough to stop Finn wanting to kill me.

'JUMP!' he roared.

So I JUMPED. I pretended I was in a flying machine and I didn't mean to but I must have flapped my arms like a bird's wings on the way down and let out my secret, and as my foot went snap underneath me I screamed.

But I wasn't dead. I was still Willem Edward Smith who lived on the 18th floor, Flat 103 of the Beckham Estate, Beckham Street, North West London, NW1 7AD.

Finn started to laugh. Then they all started to laugh because Finn was laughing.

He bent close to me and hissed in my face, 'He thinks he's a frigging bird. Fly, boy, fly.'

'Oi! What do you lot think you're doing?' It was Mr Patricks the caretaker sprinting toward us.

'Run!' yelled Finn.

Finn grabbed Sasha's hand and they all ran away, leaving me on the ground with a foot that had snapped. Something glinted in the grass. It was Sasha's gold hoop earring. I reached out and grabbed it, even though it is a fact that you should not move after an accident. It hurt. I hid the earring in my pocket. It was evidence that Sasha was there when I jumped off the wall and I did not want someone who might be a friend getting into trouble.

'One day,' I shouted after them. 'One day I'll fly.'

2

Sasha

If Finn Mason shouts 'run', you run as fast as you can or you're dead. I wouldn't call it running though. I'd call it dragging, pulling me across the playground like that.

Laurence and TJ were faster than us. I saw them grab a bag of chips off this shrimp of a boy in Year Seven, who lives on the Tarkey House Estate, and run off laughing. There will be big trouble. Thieving chips causes battles and the Tarkey Crew (or T Crew, as they like to be called), and the Beckham Street Boyz are at war.

'Come on, Sash,' Finn shouted. 'There ain't no way I'm getting chucked out of school again. RUN.'

He dragged me further away from Willem and he held my hand so tight it hurt. SOMETIMES I HATE FINN.

So it wasn't exactly as if I had any choice in the matter.

Except, if I'm being pure truthful with myself, I did have a choice and I chose to run.

The bell blasted my eardrums. Friday afternoon, time for double Maths with Mrs Hubert. What a messed-up day.

Finn pulled me into the classroom, to our usual place at the back on the right side, 'cause the left side is T Crew territory. Mrs Hubert was at the front, writing rubbish sums on the white board.

At the beginning of term Mrs Hubert did a friendship scheme and tried to mix us up, but her hair went grey trying. She just don't get it. I don't think she gets out much.

Richie Lane and Finn were giving each other evils across the classroom. Then Mrs Hubert turns and, in her most sarky voice, goes, 'Finn, how do you plan to write your sums down without a pen? Are you going to write with your finger?'

Then she gave me one of her 'AFTER YOUR TERM OF DISRUPTIVE BEHAVIOUR YOU ARE ON YOUR LAST CHANCE, SASHA BARTON' looks.

Last chance one: for texting Finn in class when he

was sitting next to me. Which if you ask me is blatantly unfair, as how else was I meant to communicate with him when she wouldn't let us talk?

Last chance two: for daydreaming out of the window, gazing up at the clouds. According to Mrs Hubert I had missed a piece of vital Maths information that was imperative to my future – which I very much doubt.

She doesn't half exaggerate.

So now I am on chance three, which I do not want to lose 'cause it would mean a letter home to Dad, who would probably forget to read it, then people would stick their noses in, and I might get chucked out of school and end up with my arch enemy Malisha down the pupil referral unit. THIS I DO NOT WANT TO HAPPEN.

I tried to work out the sums on the white board, honest I did. But in my head I was still running. Finn was scrabbling for a pen in his bag. I ignored him and tried to make sense of the muddled numbers on the white board.

He elbowed me in the ribs. 'Give us one of yours,' he hissed.

I gave him my best sky-blue gel pen. He'd

better not lose it.

My feelings are all jumbled up about Finn. It's been me and Finn friends together for ever since we used to play in the sandpit at nursery. Then two weeks ago he just reached out and held my hand, and my fingers were on fire, and this tiny jumping bean started to jiggle around in my tummy and I told myself I was being proper draft – but these feelings just grew and grew and I couldn't stop them and he looked at me and my knees went funny and I actually imagined what it would be like to kiss Finn, only I am not going to do that – not yet.

Sometimes I proper love him, but sometimes, like today, I hate him. How could he force someone to jump off a mega-high wall and then just run away like that?

And not just someone. Willem, who is cute in a nerdy sort of way. Willem, who never hurt no one, not ever. Not like Finn, who lives to cause pain.

Then it smacked me. I had run away. I had laughed just 'cause Finn had. I was as bad, leaving Willem in a mashed-up heap on the floor. I hated myself. I made up my mind then and there to try to be a better person.

Then there was a knock on the door and the

headteacher, Mr Richardson, marched in and I swear my heart stopped. He whispered something in Mrs Hubert's ear and I thought: this is it. Willem's grassed. He's named and shamed and Finn will go to young offenders' and I will be excluded for being there when Finn made him jump off that wall and . . . and . . . I am finished. I felt dizzy and in my head I was still running.

Then that shrimpy kid knocks on the door, the one TJ and Laurence robbed the chips off, and says, 'Mr Richardson, the ambulance has arrived,' and Mr Richardson stormed out.

Mrs Hubert started stomping up and down, screaming and shouting, 'What I would like to know is how did Willem get up on to the top of the wall? He did not get up by himself, did he?'

Blah blah blah BLAH BLAH.

The whole class suddenly pretended they were finding the sums on the white board terribly interesting, but Mrs Hubert kept shooting Finn vicious laser looks with her eyes.

'Poor Willem has badly injured his foot and has been taken to hospital. I think it would be nice if someone showed him some friendship.'

And before I knew it, I had stuck my hand in the air.

'I will, Miss,' I shouted out.

Finn kicked my chair leg hard under the desk and hissed, 'You dare.' And he kept saying it, 'You dare, you dare, you dare.' And kicking and kicking and kicking . . .

But I do dare and I put my hand over my ears to block out his words and that was when I realized one of my gold hoop earrings had gone.

They're my favourites. It's no more than I deserve. It's my punishment for letting Finn drag me away from Willem like that.

My chair nearly tipped over with an extra fierce kick and one too many 'You dare's'. My head was busting and I couldn't take it no more. I NEEDED URGENT HEAD SPACE AWAY FROM FINN.

With a jerk in my gut, I knew that I had to be at home right now to sort this situation out in my head and in my heart, and before I knew it I was up and running out of the classroom shouting, 'Miss, Miss, my earring's gone. I've got to find it. They was the last thing my mum ever gave me before she left.'

WHICH WAS A BLATANT LIE.

As if my mum would give me a massive gold hoop earring before she abandoned me when I was three. I got the earrings from Camden Market.

I could feel Finn's eyes burning my back as I ran out of the classroom, but I just kept on running.

I didn't care that I am on my last chance with Mrs Hubert. I kept on running anyway. I ran past the flattened patch on the grass where Willem had landed and it made my gut punch the floor.

Something sticking out of the grass caught my eye. It was that model Spitfire Mrs Hubert lets Willem spin the propeller of in Maths. She says it HELPS HIM – which if you ask me is blatantly unfair since she has confiscated my mobile seven times this term, and texting my friends HELPS ME get through her boring lessons. But since I am trying to be a better person, I swooped the model plane into my pocket to give to Willem.

I ran round the back of the girls' changing rooms and squeezed through the forbidden gap in the fence, and ran and ran and ran away from school, towards Beckham Street and my flat, Number Sixty-one Beckham Estate.

It was sweaty running in the mad March sun. I had no breath left and a stabbing stitch in my side by the time I reached the wasteland by our flats. I dragged myself across it, over the scrubby burned-out grass and busted goalpost and the bench that someone had turned upside down long ago, and I jumped over the ditch and past the proper gigantic hut that used to be the youth club before it got shut down, and reached the edge of the massive courtyard that was in front of our flats. The whole place was in chaos. There were two removal lorries parked outside Number One. Old cars were being pulled down the slope into the space under our block, 'cause it's on stilts, see. You can walk right under our flats. Carpenters and builders were everywhere, making a proper racket. I looked up and they were hammering up this big blue sign that said:

Changing Gear Garage Project

I was looking up at the sign as I walked towards the flats' entrance when – smack! I banged into this old man with sticking-up white hair. He dropped the box he was carrying. 'Sorry,' I said before he could cuss me and I tried to pick up the box, but it was too heavy.

He never even moaned, he just laughed and said, 'It's quite all right, my dear,' and his eyes were twinkly stars in the sky. He picked up the box, like it weighed nothing, did a little hop and a skip and carried it into Number One. There was something about him that made lightness tickle my heart. Just for a second before I felt proper stressed again.

I held my breath in the smelly lift to the eighth floor, which is as far as the stupid lift will go since the T Crew messed with the lift buttons. Then I had to run all the way up the steps to the eleventh floor to reach Flat Sixty-one where I live.

I put my key in the lock. I could hear Dad playing some riffs on his guitar.

Dad's called Fox, by the way. He used to be famous. He played lead guitar in the band Zebra Blue. Then the band had a bust-up, and their dodgy record producer ran off with all the money, and Dad and I ended up living on the Beckham Estate. Don't worry if you haven't heard of Zebra Blue. They were big way back. It's wrinkly music. Proper embarrassing, if you ask me. My dad's real name is Kevin. But you don't get rock stars called Kevin, so he changed it. Dad is practically the only one still alive in Zebra Blue. The other members all died of various plane crashes, car crashes or drinking too much. Apart from Ferret, the drummer, who my mum ran off with when I was three.

Most dads would notice if their daughters arrived home too early when they were meant to be in school doing Maths, but not mine.

And while I've got this confessional thing going – when I told Finn that my dad banned me from seeing him six times this year, well, it was a blatant lie. My dad doesn't even notice when I hang out with Finn. I just tell that lie when I need urgent head space.

Flinging myself on my bed, it felt like my thoughts were busting my head. My legs were wobbly and my clothes felt sticky from all that running and my stitch was pounding. So I did what I always do when I feel rank. I CLOSED MY EYES AND PRETENDED I WAS FLYING. Over the tag-sprayed walls. Over the estate, away from the Beckham Street Boyz and the T Crew, the young ones kicking a ball, the old ones who left school and can't get jobs, sitting on street corners, mixing trouble, cussing life.

I flew higher and higher over trees – floating, floating in the air with the robins' wings brushing my cheeks and the clouds in my hair – away from Finn, away from SCHOOL, away from DADS what don't notice you. It's proper relaxing, flying.

Flying-boy Willem. I had seen him flap his arms as

17

he jumped off that wall. I've seen him do it when Finn makes him jump off desks too – a tiny flap of his fingers, but I saw it. Willem doesn't know that we share a secret.

As I flew higher, I could see Finn gliding towards me. He looked gentle and kind – like I know he can be, not like the nutter he was at school today – and he took my hand and we dipped and dived through all the years of memories we shared together and I felt pure happiness swim through me.

I came down to earth with a bump. Right, SORTED! I would go to the hospital, make sure Willem was OK and also make sure he had not grassed on Finn. THAT WAY I WAS LOOKING AFTER EVERYONE.

The clock said three forty-five! Finn would be out of school and looking for me. I didn't have much time.

Rescuing Willem's model Spitfire from my pocket, I tore off my sweaty school uniform and kicked it into the corner and yanked open my wardrobe door that won't close properly 'cause of my mega collection of vintage clothes. That's the only thing I inherited from my mum, my love of costumes. She was wardrobe assistant on Zebra Blue's tour, which is how she met my dad. I grabbed my jeans and new turquoise top and scrabbled into them, squeezing the tiny Spitfire into my front jeans pocket.

My mobile was vibrating from under the bed. It must have fallen out of my pocket when I was flying.

I clicked on the message.

Where r u? R u with Willem?
I am coming to find u. Finn

I pressed delete and threw my phone on the bed so Finn couldn't reach me.

The guitar playing got louder and twangier. I opened my bedroom door and ran down the hall.

'Hey, is that you, Sash? Come and listen to this,' yelled Dad.

'Laters, Dad,' I shouted, banging the door shut.

I had TO GET PAST FINN'S FLAT FIRST 'cause there was a chance he could be home already if he ran home from school. He lives in Flat Sixty-five, on the eleventh floor, same as me. I couldn't hear anything from inside his flat. No music banging like it normally does when Finn's home.

But just to be on the safe side I dropped to my hands and knees, trying not to mess up my new turquoise top and slowly, slowly, crawled along the balcony under Finn's kitchen window. I was nearly there. Until suddenly I was flat on my back and staring straight into the eyes of Buster, Finn's brown Staffie, and my face was being licked to death. There was a pair of pink trainers standing over me and a shopping bag dangling over my nose.

It was Trish, Finn's mum, back from the shops.

'Buster, get off her. Sasha, what are you doing on the dirty floor? Get up.'

I heard a snigger and I turned my head. Tamsin, her ginger bob sharp like her gob, and Malisha, her blonde ponytail so tight it's a wonder her eyes don't ping from their sockets, were standing at the end of the balcony with another couple of girls off our estate, pointing at me.

'That's where you belong,' shouted Malisha. 'On the floor with the dog.'

'At least I don't look like one,' I shouted back. 'This is just a temporary situation, whereas your face, Malisha, is a permanent one.'

I jumped up and knocked Trish's bag out of her hand by accident. The next thing I knew, potatoes were rolling everywhere and Buster starts chasing after them, 'cause he's a proper mental dog and loves licking raw potatoes.

'Sorry, Trish,' I yelled and ran away for the second time that day, with Buster following, barking and making a show of me.

I pushed through the girls and belted along the balcony and down the stairs just as Finn, TJ and Laurence were coming up.

They blocked my way.

'Have you been with Willem?' said Finn.

'No,' I said.

'Why did you run off like that?' said Finn. 'Mrs Hubert went off on one like a mentalist.'

'You were doing my head in,' I said.

Finn laughed, he put his arm around me and pulled me to him and gave me that look that makes my knees go funny.

'Come to ours,' said Finn. 'We're going to watch that film, *Battle of Britain*.'

Now I've got to level with you. I nearly wobbled in my FIND WILLEM MISSION, I nearly did, 'cause I love that old film with all those Spitfire planes. It's my favourite, my joint number one, along with *Hope and Glory*, 'cause I've a thing for nineteen-forties vintage clothes.

'Come on, Sash, my mum's making chips,' said Finn.

At the word 'chips', Buster jumped up and knocked Finn down the stairs and I snatched this opportunity to run through the gap. TJ and Laurence's mouths hung open like muppets as I JUMPED over Finn.

I LOVE THAT DOG.

I ran down to the 8th floor and pressed the lift button over and over again. I could hear the lift whirring up as Finn was running down the stairs after me. The lift opened and I jumped in, but Finn put his foot in the door to stop it closing.

'Sash, come and have some chips with us.'

'Finn, stop ordering me around.' I JUMPED on his foot hard. He moved it and the door closed. As the lift started going down I heard Finn banging on the door.

'You'd better not be going to the hospital to see Willem!' he screamed

'I'M GOING TO THE HOSPITAL TO MAKE SURE HE DOESN'T GRASS, YOU FOOL,' I screamed back.

But I got a mouth full of putrid air 'cause the lift reeked of wee. I did my holding-my-breath thing and tried to think of nice things, which I always try to do in this stinking lift. But I couldn't think of nice things. All I could think of was Trish making chips with potatoes that Buster had licked all over, and I felt sick.

When the lift bumped to a stop, I ran out and down the street and over the Heath to the hospital to say sorry to Willem, the boy who loves to fly. I reckon Willem is one of life's special people.

3

WILLEM

'I would like to go home please,' I said to the stranger lady, Rosemary from social services.

I have said I would like to go home 8 times.

My right foot throbbed and my left big toe stung.

Rosemary, the stranger lady with red hair and 6 grey hairs in her fringe, leaned too close to me. She smelled of garlic.

So I shut my eyes and counted to 10, and I flew out of my wheelchair and through the ceiling of the hospital and up, up into the sky. The clouds tickled my cheeks. I ducked and dived through a flock of geese flying towards me. The pain stopped. I was free.

'Uh humph,' coughed Rosemary.

I bumped back down into my wheelchair.

'Oh dear, are you tired?' she said. 'This is all a bit much for you, isn't it, Willem?'

I opened my eyes a fraction and squinted at Rosemary. My plaster cast on my right foot looked like a big fat cloud through my eyelashes, but inside it was not rainwater but a fractured foot that throbbed.

I opened my eyes fully.

'No, I am not tired,' I said. 'You are too close to me and I do not like garlic.'

'Oh,' said Rosemary, and her face went red like her hair.

Her bleeper bleeped for the 10th time and she sighed for the 11th.

'Willem, are you being bullied?' she said very slowly with her mouth opening too wide. She had 4 fillings and spinach caught between her front teeth.

Rosemary Stranger Lady talked to me like a stupid person. I ignored her and thought of an aeronautical formula in my head.

Match number $M = \underline{V}/a$ Where V = the speed of the plane

and a = speed of sound = 340 m/sec

(M is supersonic for $1.2 < M < 4$)

A man shouted rude words outside in the corridor. He must have had too much to drink.

'You are proper rude, you are,' a girl's voice shouted back.

I do not like shouting.

My fingers started to jiggle.

'I need to go home now. I need to give my gran her evening cup of tea and a digestive biscuit, when she comes home from the 65 Club. She will be sad that her grandson, Willem Edward Smith, has a bit of him fractured. I need to make her happy with tea.'

The door moved a crack. Someone was listening.

'Our lift does not go up to the 18th floor where I live. It only goes to floor 8. It is going to take me a long time with a fractured foot to get the 92 bus and get up to the 18th floor of the Beckham Estate to make my gran her cup of tea. You must let me go now.'

From the left corner of my eye I saw the door move again and a bit of black hair and turquoise material poked through.

Rosemary sighed for the 12th time.

I could see a brown eye peeping through the

crack of the door.

'Willem, your gran cannot look after you with a fractured foot, a cut big toe and no lift. We are trying to get hold of her but no one is answering the phone at the 65 Club. We need somewhere for you to stay tonight. My colleague is phoning round our emergency foster carers.'

My breath started to flutter faster and faster.

I must live higher than the birds with my gran, not in a stranger house on the ground.

The door banged open.

Sasha Barton leaped in.

'Willem, I came as fast as I could. He's my cousin, Miss,' she said to Rosemary.

She flung her arms round me. Her bumps knocked my cheek.

I opened my mouth to explain to Sasha that she had got it wrong, that I do not have any cousins who live on the Beckham Estate. But Sasha whispered, 'Shut UP.

'Willem is staying at ours tonight. I'd best get him home. Thanks, Miss,' she said and she started to push my wheelchair out of the door.

'Stop.' Rosemary started flicking through her

papers. 'There is no mention of any other family members in the notes apart from—'

'1 gran, who I live with, and 1 mother, Amy Smith, who could not cope with me and moved to Bristol,' I finished for her.

'But I'm a relative too,' said Sasha.

'I can't just let Willem go with you.' Rosemary had a frowning face on.

'My dad, who is Willem's uncle, is talking to the doctor at reception. They want to talk to you urgently. They asked me to tell you,' said Sasha.

'Why didn't they phone me?'

Sasha shrugged her shoulders. 'That doctor looked vexed. You had better be quick, Miss.'

'You 2 stay here,' said Rosemary and ran out of the door.

'Quick,' said Sasha. 'We need to escape now.'

'You told a lie, Sasha. I am not your cousin,' I said.

'Big blatant lies,' laughed Sasha. 'Come on, let's get you home to your gran.' She started to push me out of the room.

A bang, a crash, a scream. The drunk man said the rudest word ever and a woman shouted, 'Help!'

There was an upturned table and broken chairs and everyone was staring at the drunk man, who was being held by 2 men in blue jumpers with badges that said *Security* on them. Rosemary had slipped on to her bottom as she tried to step over the water leaking from the cooler. A nurse was trying to help her up.

Sasha turned right and quickly pushed me away from the angry people, down a long, long corridor, then we burst through swing doors out into the open air and we were free.

We started to laugh as Sasha pushed me faster and faster and faster, over the Heath until we were flying and the birds were squawking and the dogs were barking.

One bark was louder than the rest, then Buster, who is Finn's brown Staffordshire bull terrier, came running up to me. My fingers jiggled. I do not like it when mammals get too close. Buster jumped on my lap. My body shook. He licked my cheek. His dog kiss was warm. He did not smell of garlic. He smelled like lovely salty chips and he had kindness in his eyes. Maybe Buster can be my new friend.

'Buster, have you followed me, boy? Come on

then, do you want a ride?' said Sasha. Buster barked and wagged his tail. Sasha giggled and she gave the dog a kiss.

Sasha huffed and puffed as she pushed the chair with me and Buster up to the top of Parliament Hill. Rude people turned and stared. I don't think they had seen a dog in a wheelchair before.

When we reached the top, Buster jumped off my knees and ran round in circles barking. Sasha whirled round with her arms out like wings.

'I'm flying,' she shouted. 'As high as the birds.'

'Higher,' I said, as I looked down at a miniature St Paul's Cathedral and London Eye.

Sasha bent down and whispered in my ear.

'You do it too, don't you? Go flying. I've seen you flap your arms when you jump.'

'Yes,' I whispered and held out my arm wings.

Sasha grabbed my hand and we shut our eyes and flew together. 2 birds touching wings. Then she flung herself on the grass, giggling, and we looked up at the clouds.

I could hear a whirring sound. I looked round. A miniature motor aeroplane, an exact copy of the Wright brothers' glider number 3 built in 1902, was swooping among the treetops.

There was an old man with white sticking-up hair holding the control box.

Sasha sat up and waved at him.

'I bumped into him on our estate,' said Sasha. 'I knocked a box he was carrying out of his hands.'

The old man waved back and did a little jig, kicking his legs in the air. Sasha laughed.

'Oh,' she said, reaching into her pocket, 'nearly forgot. I found it in the grass,' and she put my model Spitfire Mark 1 into my hand. I spun the propeller fast. I felt happy.

I put my model Spitfire Mark 1 safely into my right pocket. I took her gold hoop earring out of my left pocket and held it out to her.

'I kept it safe,' I said.

'Oh Willem, they're my favourites. You star.'

I was not sure if she meant a star in the galaxy or a person who is famous, which I am not, except to my gran.

Sasha kissed me on the cheek. My body shook. I do not like being kissed, even by my gran. Yet her lips felt soft. Sasha has brown eyes. I think this was a nice kiss.

'Are you my friend?' I asked her. I had to be sure.

'Course I am, Willem,' she said. 'I am proper sorry I laughed and ran away.'

'Finn dragged you,' I said.

'I should have stayed,' she said. 'I had a choice.'

Mrs Hubert will be very happy. I have done ½ of my homework by making 1 friend of my own age. I looked at the tiny cars in the distance stopping at the traffic lights. I like the order of traffic lights. Red. Red and amber. Green. Amber. Red. They make me feel safe because I know what is coming next.

Sasha is my amber friend. Amber means caution. Green means go. My green friends are the friends that go with me through the days, minutes and seconds of my life. They are friends that Mrs Hubert does not count: Bernie from Bernie's Burger Bar, Gran – and now Buster, because I don't think Mrs Hubert would count a dog as a friend of my own age. I have made Buster a green friend immediately because he is a dog and will not say words that hurt me. Red means stop. Red is for danger. Finn, TJ and Laurence are red people. Finn is the brightest red of all. Gran says that all the boys in the Beckham Street Boyz and T Crew are red people. She said I must not go near them, which is very hard when some of the members are in my class and the Beckham Street Boyz live on my estate. Gran does not know what it is like to be young because she is old.

'Sasha, I need to go home to my gran now. I have to get her a cup of tea and a digestive biscuit. You can have one too.'

Sasha jumped up. 'Come on, we'll fly down the hill. Are you ready?'

'Yes,' I said.

Buster jumped back on my knee, barking. He was squashing my legs. Sasha grabbed hold of the handles of my wheelchair and pushed hard and then we were flying faster and faster.

Then I saw them, waiting for us at the bottom of the hill: Finn, TJ and Laurence. I had my arms tight round Buster. I dug my fingers into his fur to stop them jiggling. Faster and faster we flew towards them.

We couldn't stop.

4

WILLEM

Sasha screamed. I do not like screaming. I could feel her pulling back on the handles, trying to stop the wheelchair. But Sasha is not strong enough to stop 1 wheelchair hurtling down a hill, with 1 boy and 1 Staffordshire bull terrier sitting in it.

My cheeks were blowing back and I was flying through the air towards danger.

I held my arms tighter around my new dog-friend Buster, to stop him jumping off my knees and getting a fractured foot too. Finn, TJ and Laurence were getting nearer and nearer. I closed my eyes so I could not see them. I counted to 10.

The wheelchair stopped.

I opened my eyes. Finn's face was right in front of mine, his 7 freckles nearly touching my nose. He had his snarling face on.

'Stay away from my dog,' he spat.

A drop of spit landed on my trousers. Finn grabbed hold of Buster's dog collar and yanked him off my knees. Buster yelped and pulled away from Finn and hid behind Sasha.

'Leave Willem alone,' said Sasha, and she stood up and gave Finn a push and stuck her bumps and chin out. She had her ferocious face on.

'Did you grass, Willem?' Finn grabbed hold of her wrist. 'Did you, Sasha? Did either of you tell the teachers that we were there when you jumped off the wall? 'Cause if you did, you're dead.'

'Grass is what you are standing on. It is not telling truths to a teacher,' I said.

'ARE YOU TRYING TO BE FUNNY?' screamed Finn, a second dot of spit jumping on to my trousers.

'No, I am not very good at jokes,' I said. 'I do not understand them.'

'FINN, LEAVE WILLEM ALONE,' said Sasha, freeing her wrist from Finn's grasp. 'You know he takes everything dead literal. You know that.'

'What did you 2 tell the doctors at that hospital? Am I going to be chucked out of school?'

'For your information,' said Sasha, 'Willem was dead brave. He never said nothing. Not one word about you. I know 'cause I was listening at the door.'

'They were going to take me away from my gran,' I said. 'Make me live with strangers. But I did not tell them I was being bullied.'

'Who are you calling bullies?' said Laurence.

'Yeah,' said TJ. 'We ain't bullies.'

Then they grabbed hold of my chair and started rocking it.

Laurence's shaved head scraped my cheek and I saw he had a tomato sauce stain on his grey hoodie.

TJ's real name is Thomas-John and his mother, Aunty Lou, who is not my real aunty, is from Jamaica. She goes to St Bartholomew's church with my gran. TJ has a swirly pattern shaved into his hair.

It's funny, isn't it, the things that go through your mind when you are being rocked in a wheelchair.

'Jump! Jump! Jump!' they screamed, their faces too close to mine, Finn's 7 freckles wriggling in front of my eyes.

I obviously could not jump as my right foot has a fracture and the left big toe has a deep cut in it. I shook my bottom around a bit and hoped that was enough. My foot hurt and I thought I was going to sick up the cheese and tomato sandwich the lady in the hospital gave me from the trolley.

As my chair tilted to the right I saw a boy's face behind a tree. He had a yellow bandana tied round his mouth and a Staffordshire bull terrier at his side. I thought it was Richie Lane from Tarkey House, but when you are being shaken about in a wheelchair it is hard to tell.

As my chair tilted to the left I saw more boys with yellow bandanas tied round their mouths, hiding behind trees with their dogs.

Sasha's face kept bobbing up in between Finn and TJ's shoulders. She was shouting at them to stop. Her face was twisted, her arms thrusting in the gaps between their bodies. I think she was trying to grab my wheelchair, but she grabbed my hand instead. I held Sasha's hand tight as they screamed, 'Jump! Jump! Jump!' I think she was trying to pull me towards her, but I was trapped.

'How can you do this to someone like Willem? I

HATE YOU, FINN!' screamed Sasha. Her bottom lip was shaking.

My wheelchair rocked faster and faster. I held Sasha's hand tighter. 'Jump! Jump! Jump!' they screamed.

Finn grabbed hold of Sasha's turquoise top and tried to pull her arm so that we could not hold hands. There was a ripping sound.

Then a whirring cut through the air, getting louder and louder, then nearer and nearer. Finn shouted, 'DUCK!' and my chair stopped rocking. The boys and Sasha threw themselves on the ground as the miniature motor plane, a copy of the Wright brothers' glider number 3 built in 1902, that we had seen the old man fly at the top of the hill, ducked and dived through them again and again, just missing them by centimetres. It swooped just above my head and landed on my lap. The plane was not damaged.

I looked over my shoulder. The old man with sticking-up hair was running down the hill towards us. He was fast.

Sasha was shaking and her turquoise top had a rip on the shoulder. I could see her pink bra strap.

She stood up and she pulled my wheelchair backwards away from Finn.

My breath was fluttering. I felt sick. I reached into my right pocket for my model Spitfire Mark 1 and spun the propeller fast. I recited an aeroplane fact in my head to calm me: Turbulence is the most common cause of injury when flying.

Then Sasha fell to the ground and she was shaking and gasping for breath all at the same time.

'Sasha,' said Finn, 'I didn't mean to . . .' and he tried to pull her up off the ground.

'DON'T TOUCH ME!' she screamed.

'Step away from her,' said a voice. I turned round. The old man had reached the bottom of the hill. 'You've done enough damage.'

The old man kneeled down next to Sasha on the grass.

'My name is Archie,' he said.

He showed us a badge that said: *Beckham Estate Community Project Manager* next to a picture of him.

'We live there,' I said, 'so that means you are our new neighbour. It means that you are not a stranger.'

'It does indeed,' said Archie. His eyes twinkled and the corners of his mouth twitched, which is what people do when they are nearly smiling.

'I am Willem and this is my new friend Sasha.'

'Pleased to make your acquaintance,' he said, and he gave Sasha a handkerchief.

'Come on, my dear, let's cover you up,' he said, and he took his jacket off and put it over Sasha's shoulders. Archie then started saying, 'Breathe in and breath out,' till Sasha was calmer. Then he gave her some water from a bottle in his bag.

Archie ran his hand through his sticking-up hair. 'From what I saw up there, you're a very brave young lady.'

'She tried to help me. I couldn't jump,' I said.

'I saw everything,' he said.

'Sometimes it's hard,' sniffed Sasha.

'Dealing with all those boys,' whispered Archie.

Sasha nodded. 'I just wanted them to stop,' she hiccupped, 'but they wouldn't listen.'

I spun the propeller of my Spitfire fast.

I turned my head round. Finn, Laurence and TJ were standing in a huddle, gawping.

'Do you know their names?' said Archie.

'Is that grassing?' I asked.

'No, it's helping me and helping them,' said Archie.

'Oh,' I said, and whispered their names into Archie's ear.

Finn mouthed, 'You're dead.' I spun my Spitfire propeller faster and faster.

Archie snatched some business cards out of his pocket and marched towards the boys and thrust one each in their hands.

'Finn, Laurence and TJ, I want you to report to me at the new Community Project in the garage under the Beckham Estate, after school tomorrow. I'll get you mending cars, not breaking people's lives. If you don't turn up I'll go to the police and report you. Is that understood?'

Finn, TJ and Laurence had their scared faces on, just for 1 second, before they put their hard faces back on.

Archie handed me a card. It was blue, with a picture of a Vintage Ford Model T on it. Above the picture in gold writing it said: Changing Gears Community Garage Project. Mend cars – don't steal them.

I put the card into my right pocket with my model Spitfire Mark 1.

'Now get out of my sight,' said Archie to Finn, TJ and Laurence, 'and I'll see you tomorrow.'

I watched as they strolled away from us, my new green friend, Buster, trotting behind them, wagging his tail.

All of a sudden the boys with yellow bandanas tied over their mouths jumped out from the trees with their snarling dogs in front of Finn, TJ and Laurence. It was the T Crew.

Their path was blocked.

5

Sasha

I was feeling Finn's fear as the T Crew closed in on him.

All my HATE vanished.

'NO,' I screamed from my belly, but no sound came out.

I stumbled forward a few steps, then my legs froze.

'Sasha, you must stay with me,' said Willem. 'You promised to take me home to my gran.'

His words bounced off me.

Finn, TJ and Laurence clenched their fists, trying to look hard. Trying to look like there were more than three of them, as they were surrounded by the T Crew and their Staffies.

'Please do something,' I screeched to Archie, 'cause even though he is a proper old man, he is strong and fast.

'There are too many of them. I'm going to phone the police,' said Archie, scrabbling in his bag for his phone.

I don't know why, right, 'cause I can look after myself, but I suddenly wanted my dad urgently, to tell him what was happening. I reached for my phone to call him, but my pocket was empty. Then it smacked me! I had thrown it on the bed in a strop, after Finn had texted me.

Archie found his phone and started to dial.

Richie stepped up close to Finn.

'You don't understand, either of you. The police won't get here in time. FINN'S GOING TO GET MASHED UP!' I screamed.

If they were on the estate with the rest of the Beckham Street Boyz for backup, maybe they would stand a chance. But here on the Heath in the middle of nowhere, they would get slaughtered. Finn was the leader at school. Finn was a valuable prize. So if the T Crew got him, they'd won. Richie's dog, Nasher, barked at Buster, who ran howling to hide behind Finn. He's not into gangs, Buster. He's into cuddles.

The scream in my belly freed itself. 'FINN, NOOOO,

PLEASE!' and I ran towards him.

Archie grabbed me, but I wriggled free.

Then as I reached them, Richie Lane gave the nod and all the T Crew took off their yellow bandanas and threw them on the grass. Even the dogs stopped barking. They were calling a truce. I stood dead still.

Finn stepped forwards and held his fist out and punched it in the air, touching Richie's: fist to fist, gang to gang communicating.

'We've been sent to fetch you,' said Richie, 'by the Beckham Street and Tarkey Crew elders.'

My heart stopped ticking. If the gang leaders wanted to speak to them, this meant something serious was brewing.

I didn't like it.

'Finn,' I said, 'come on, let's get out of here.'

'Stay out of this, Sash,' shouted Finn.

'Tell her to go,' said Richie. 'I aint talking my business in front of Sasha.'

Finn grabbed hold of Buster's collar and my wrist, and pulled us away from the others.

'Let go of my arm, Finn,' I hissed.

'I'm begging you, Sash, take Buster home. Get out of here now.'

He took Buster's lead out of his pocket, clipped it to his collar and put the end in my hand.

'Please, Finn,' I said, pleading into his eyes. 'Don't go attracting more trouble.'

'I thought you hated me,' said Finn.

'I do hate you,' I said, 'for what you've done to Willem, but you've got right under my skin, Finn. It's you and me together for ever. And I don't want you hurt.'

Finn pulled me to him, held me proper tight for a second, then walked away. All the boys whistled, making a show of me. THE FOOLS.

Finn and Richie muttered their business to each other real quiet. A few words trickled into my ears. '. . . Join in . . . us . . . together . . . No fights, we've got to help . . .'

I couldn't hear any more, even though my ears were wagging. Then Finn, TJ and Laurence reached into their pockets and tied their purple bandanas around their mouths and the T Crew reached for their yellow bandanas and all the boys ran off together, with Finn and Richie leading the way.

I grabbed hold of Buster's lead tight, but he yanked away from me and pulled me down flat on the grass and broke free.

'Buster,' I screamed, 'come back here,' 'cause I don't want him being involved in gang activity. But he ignored me. He is proper disobedient, that dog.

I felt a pair of arms lift me to my feet. It was Archie.

'Did you see?' I said.

'The truce ritual? Yes, my dear, I did.'

'Did you call the police?' I asked.

Archie shook his head. 'No signal – and no point when I saw they weren't going to fight.'

'I don't like it,' I muttered. 'Something's happening.'

'In the meantime,' said Archie, 'there is a young man over there who could do with your friendship.'

I looked at Willem sitting there, sad in his wheelchair. His fingers were doing this shaking thing, wiggling about. He does this when he gets stressed. I nodded.

'I will try to be a good friend,' I said.

As we walked back to Willem there was silence, apart from a crow hawking and a breeze through the trees. Noises you can only hear when there ain't nothing else. It was just me and Willem and old man Archie. I felt fear in my gut for Finn.

When I reached Willem he turned a funny colour

and leaned over the side of his chair and was sick. He looked so ashamed it cut my heart.

It was gross. Usually I would have vanished out of the situation, but seeing as I am trying to be a better person and not the kind that runs away from people with injured feet, I acted proper mature and gave Willem the rest of the bottle of water that Archie had given me earlier.

'It's OK,' I said, 'honest,' and I smiled at him. I stretched out my hand and touched his cheek. Willem flinched, so I pulled his chair away to some clean grass.

Willem started stroking the wings of the motor aeroplane in his lap like it was a cat. His fingers had stopped wiggling.

'I am glad you stayed, Sasha. We will have a cup of tea when we get to my gran's.'

I knew then with THE WHOLE OF MY HEART, as I looked at the hope painted on Willem's face, that I Sasha, had to finish what I had started. I had to get this strange, special boy who shared my secret wish to fly, back safe to his gran.

'We need to check this chair over,' said Archie and he kneeled down and started to run his fingers slowly over the wheel spokes and tighten screws.

I sat on the grass and looked up at the sky. A police helicopter sliced through the air above us, dipping and diving, making a racket as it raved through the clouds. I felt jumpy. I wanted to get home. But Archie was taking LIKE FOR EVER to fix the wheelchair.

I shivered and pulled Archie's jacket tight around my shoulders. The tweed made my arms scratchy. The jacket smelled of oil and melted chocolate. But there was another smell. It was smoke. There was smoke in the breeze.

After what seemed like years we were ready to make our way over the Heath. Archie wheeled Willem, slow and careful. My feet were twitching for home, so I ran a little way ahead, but my lungs started to itch and my eyes water 'cause the smoke in the breeze was getting thicker. I turned the corner at the oak tree and stepped off the Heath, on to the main road that leads to the Beckham Estate.

I stopped, paralyzed.

Cars were lying on their sides, burning. The road was sprinkled with broken glass. War whoops filled the air. Boys and girls with yellow and purple bandanas were throwing stones. My eyes searched for Finn, but I couldn't see him.

Now it all clicked in my brain. The elders of the Beckham Street Boyz and T Crew had called a truce so they could riot together. They had called on the young ones, Finn and Richie, to come and join them.

In front of us was a line of police, wearing plastic helmets and carrying shields and truncheons, making its way slowly to our estate, shouting at people to move on or get back.

'Archie,' I screamed, 'THEY'RE RIOTING.' I heard the chair wheel up behind me.

Archie whispered. 'Please no. Not this.' He looked so sad. It smashed my heart. Ever since the youth club closed and all the jobless ones grew in number – it was like our estate had this anger sickness, bubbling away. You could feel it in the air and now it had exploded into this.

I felt a hand reach into mine. It was Willem. I closed my fist over his to stop his wiggling fingers.

Then, together as one, we both held out our arm wings.

'Shut your eyes,' I said. 'Feel the clouds in your hair and the robins' wings brush your cheeks.'

Willem's fingers wiggled faster.

'Fly,' I said. 'Come on, fly.'

But then a car exploded. We couldn't fly away from this.

6

WILLEM

We could not fly. We were trapped on the ground. The smell and heat of the explosion trickled up my nose and made my lungs sting. I wanted my gran. I felt sick. All I could see were blue legs. 26 pairs of policemen's blue legs. They were too close. I do not like it when strangers get too close.

'Righty-ho,' said Archie. 'This is the plan, my dears. Keep calm and stick together. 1 step at a time and we will soon have you back with your gran.'

My breath started to flutter as fast as a robin trapped in a net. I reached into my right pocket with my jiggling fingers for my model Spitfire Mark 1.

Archie wheeled me past a burning Peugeot 207. It made me cough.

There was screaming and shouting and banging and stones being thrown and – and – and I did what I always do when too many bad noises come at me: I started to shut down and my world went grey and started to melt. I put my hands over my ears to shut out the planet . . . but Sasha did not let go of my hand. Archie wheeled me into Beckham Street and past the 5 shops and the library at the side of the Beckham Estate.

Bernie's Burger Bar, where I get a number 2 meal (chips and chicken wings) had no door. The sign explaining the different meals you can get from 1 to 7 was lying in the middle of the road. Bernie, my green friend, was sitting in the broken doorway with his head in his hands next to a pile of squashed chips and tomato sauce. I took my hands away from my ears.

I like Bernie, he *is* my friend, even though Mrs Hubert says it does not count. He always gives me my meal number 2 with chips in 1 box and chicken wings in the other. I do not like food to touch.

'Bernie,' I shouted, 'it's me, Willem,' but he did not look up.

We passed the 90p shop which has things

for £1.50 in it so it should not be called the 90p shop. Richie Lane was in the window, with 4 big men wearing black balaclavas, taking all the items on display.

Next door, the bookmaker's door hung off its hinges. I could see a television dangling from the wall. The news was on, showing riots on other estates in London. A pair of hands in black gloves pulled down the TV and carried it out through the door. It was TJ.

Sasha ran up to him. 'TJ, what are you doing, robbing stuff? Your mum will kill you.'

TJ had his scared face on for 1 second and then laughed and pushed past us.

Sasha shouted after him, 'And where is Finn? You tell him I want words with him.'

'Come on,' said Archie. 'Remember, 1 step at a time.'

The Smart & Fast sports shop had no door and only 1 blue-and-white trainer left, lying in the middle of the smashed-up shop. The library was untouched. I do not think the riot people wanted to read books.

We reached Mr Patel's newsagent on the corner.

It had no windows, no newspapers and no sweets. Mrs Patel was kneeling on the floor. Her hands were held up to the sky and she was making a howling noise. Mr Patel was trying to help her up, but he was shaking. Sasha ran into the shop to help Mr Patel lift her off the ground, but she was not strong enough, so she kneeled amongst the broken glass, even though this is a very dangerous thing to do. Sasha put her arms round Mrs Patel to hug her.

Archie wheeled me into the shop. He righted a chair that was upside down and lifted Mrs Patel into it.

Mrs Patel grabbed Sasha's arm. 'Finn,' she said. 'Finn . . .' But she could not finish her sentence.

My gran says that is called *swallowing your words* – though you cannot swallow words because words are not food.

'Where is he?' cried Sasha. 'Did he do this?'

Mrs Patel tried to speak again, but she started to cough.

'I've got to find Finn and stop him,' shouted Sasha.

'Sasha,' said Archie, 'you simply cannot and

must not run around in a dangerous riot looking for Finn. You'll get caught up in all this trouble. This choice could change your life for ever. Please, my dear, stay with us.'

'You don't understand, I've got to find him . . .' Sasha ran to the broken door of the shop.

I had to stop my new friend running into danger.

'If you come with us, you can have a digestive biscuit. If you go and look for Finn, strangers will get too close to you and squash you and a policeman will arrest you,' I said.

Sasha turned round slowly and walked back to me.

'I've promised to get you back to your gran and I will,' Sasha said and she grabbed the handles and wheeled me out of the shop.

I felt happy. Then I felt fear.

As we turned the corner to reach the courtyard at the front of the Beckham Estate, our pathway was blocked by a big group of angry people. Some of them were shouting at the police. Some of them were shouting at the riot people. The police kept bellowing, 'GET BACK. MOVE ON.'

'Keep calm and stick together,' said Archie.

'LET US THROUGH, PLEASE,' screamed Sasha.

Sasha did not look very calm.

'WHEELCHAIR COMING THROUGH,' bellowed Archie.

When the angry people saw my fractured foot they made a gap to let my wheelchair pass. My fingers jiggled faster.

Sasha pushed me through the crowd with Archie walking next to my wheelchair. I shut my eyes. People were too close. My brain tangled but I had to get back to my gran and give her a cup of tea and a plate of digestive biscuits. She must be back from the 65 Club by now.

I opened my eyes. We had reached the edge of the crowd. In front of me was the riot.

There were Beckham Street boys running around with purple bandanas tied round their mouths and T Crew boys with the same in yellow. There were men wearing black balaclavas shouting and throwing bottles. There were some girls too, running by with their arms full of trainers looted from the Fast & Smart sports shop.

Archie shouted, 'NO. PLEASE. NO,' and leaped forwards as a group of boys with yellow bandanas rocked a Nissan Micra till it was on its side then set it on fire. 2 BMWs were overturned, already burning.

'Are those cars from your garage project?' shouted Sasha.

Archie nodded. 'They were for the young people on the estate to learn about engines, not destroy them.' His face looked sad.

There were men with television cameras filming through the smoke. Laurence ran past one making a 'whoop whoop' noise in front of the lens.

'I can't see Finn. WHERE IS FINN?' Sasha shouted to him. Laurence shrugged and laughed and ran off.

'YOU FREAK,' yelled Sasha after him.

The police were putting up metal fencing to block off the gap under our block of flats.

A fire engine with flashing lights was trying to get through the crowds.

A policeman grabbed Archie's arm and pulled him back and yelled, 'They won't get the rest of your cars, not with that fence round them.'

Just then one of the BMWs exploded, sending clouds of smoke up the staircase that led to all the flats above the ground floor and to my home on the

18th floor, Flat 103 of the Beckham Estate, Beckham Street, North West London, NW1 7AD.

My gran was trapped.

7

WILLEM

'My gran,' I screamed. 'GRAN.'

'Dad! MY DAD, HE'S IN THERE,' screeched Sasha.

'Look, the fire engines are here,' said Archie. 'They'll get them out of the flats in no time.'

Firemen ran up the steps. 'Evacuate the flats. Leave your homes now,' one of them was shouting through a megaphone. I started to rock. My fingers jiggled faster and faster.

The heat from the burning cars stung my eyes.

People started coming down the stairs, coughing.

'Stay right there,' said Archie. 'I'll be back with you in a moment.' And he ran to help a lady trying to carry 2 small boys down the last few stairs.

Then out of a cloud of smoke stepped my gran.

She was waving her big black handbag at the rioters. Her lips were pursed, which is her very angry face.

'Stop this racket now!' she shouted. 'Do you hear me? What do you think you're doing, you daft lads? Setting fire to cars, putting us all in danger.' The rioters did not listen to my gran, but the men with television cameras did and began to film her.

'Gran,' I said, waving at her. 'Gran,' I said, in my loudest voice. 'IT'S ME, YOUR GRANDSON, WILLEM EDWARD SMITH. I HAVE COME HOME TO MAKE YOU A CUP OF TEA.'

Gran stopped shouting and marched through the riot, swinging her handbag, towards us.

'Willem, thank goodness! Where've you been? There's phone messages from your school and phone messages from some woman called Rosemary saying you had escaped from hospital with your cousin. Willem, you haven't got a cousin. What's going on?'

My brain tangled and I could not speak.

Sasha stepped in front of my wheelchair.

'It was me. I took him. They were going to put him into care 'cause they said you couldn't look after him. So I helped him escape from the hospital.'

'Sasha is my new friend,' I said.

Gran stared with her mouth open at Sasha, then smiled and kissed her on the cheek.

Laurence ran past, his arms full of trainers.

'You're Fox's daughter, aren't you?' said Gran.

Sasha nodded. 'Dad, he's still in there. He's not come out.'

'Have faith,' said Gran. 'I'm sure he's on his way out right now.' She hugged Sasha as more and more people came down the stairs coughing.

Then Sasha's dad, Fox, who is very scruffy because he was a rock star and that is how rock stars dress, stepped out of the smoke with a guitar in one hand and Sasha's blue Nokia N8 in the other.

'I'M OVER HERE, DAD,' shouted Sasha, but I don't think Fox heard over the noise. He started walking in the other direction.

Sasha jumped up and down shouting, 'DAD! DAD!'

I waved my arms in the air and said in my loudest voice, 'SASHA IS HERE.'

Fox turned round and ran towards us. He grabbed Sasha's shoulders. He had a happy face on. Then he had an angry face on.

'Hey, Sash, what's the point of me buying credits for your phone if you leave it at home? That's a nuts thing to do. I've been calling and calling you. Then I found your phone on your bed.'

'What, Dad?' Sasha said. 'It took a riot for you to notice I wasn't at home?'

Fox looked very sad.

'Oh no,' said Sasha. I looked to see what she was staring at. It was Rosemary from social services pushing through the crowd towards us. She was too close. I grabbed my model Spitfire.

'That's her, that social worker from the hospital,' said Sasha, and she told Fox in quick words about helping me escape.

'We need to vanish,' said Sasha. 'Don't let her reach us.'

'I'll stand my ground and face what's coming,' said Gran.

'Are you Mrs Smith?' shouted Rosemary to my gran as she pushed past the last few people. 'Uh humph,' coughed Rosemary. 'Can I have a word?'

My world went grey and started to melt.

'Hey, can't this wait?' said Fox. 'This lady has

just had to leave her home. And in case you hadn't noticed we're in the middle of a riot.'

'I'm afraid not,' said Rosemary. She grabbed the arm of a passing policeman and showed him the identity card around her neck.

'Where is it safe for me to talk to this lady?' said Rosemary indicating my gran. 'It's urgent.'

'Come this way,' said the policeman.

'But Archie said we had to stay here,' I said, spinning and spinning and spinning the propeller of my Spitfire. Sasha pushed my chair after the policeman with Fox, Gran and Rosemary trailing behind us.

'Archie,' I shouted over my shoulder, but he was helping an old lady with a hissing ginger cat in her arms and did not hear me.

'He'll find us,' said Sasha. 'He's proper clever is Archie.'

As Sasha pushed me through the crowd, the smell, the sounds, the too-close stranger people tangled my brain. I put my hands over my ears to shut out the planet.

The policeman escorted us to the grass verge on my estate. The police vans were parked in a square and there was a large patch of grass in the middle, away from the riot.

Sasha pulled my hands away from my ears. I could not shake her hands off. She held them too tight.

'Willem, it's quiet here,' she said.

'Yes, you should be OK here,' said the policeman, then his radio crackled and he disappeared.

The crackle hurt my ears. I tried to cover them again, but Sasha would not let me.

Another van pulled up. 8 policemen climbed out, putting on their riot helmets.

'We'll speak over there, in private, away from my grandson,' said Gran to Rosemary, pointing to a patch of grass a little way away from us. 'He's had quite enough excitement for one day.'

When they had walked over to the patch of grass, Gran, Fox and Rosemary all talked at once.

Rosemary's face turned red like her hair. I tried my best to listen. I could hear 'Broken lift . . .' and 'we want what's best for Willem . . .' Fox was pointing his finger, shouting, and Gran's lips were pursed tighter. My brain tangled into tighter knots.

Gran shouted, 'YOU TAKE HIM OVER MY DEAD BODY.'

I started to whimper. Sasha rubbed my back.

'Willem, it's a saying,' she whispered. 'It don't mean she is going to die.'

I did not want to live in a stranger's house on the ground. I wanted to live higher than the birds with my gran. I curled my head into my lap and closed my eyes. I started to rock.

'Willem, look,' said Sasha.

I opened my eyes. With a hop, a skip and a run, Archie was over the grass. He stood in the middle of Gran, Fox and Rosemary. Archie started talking and waved his arms in the air like a magician and everyone just stopped talking. Fox stopped pointing his finger. Gran's lips smiled. Rosemary's face was no longer red. She shook Archie's hand and went away.

Gran put her hand on my shoulder and said in her announcing-things voice, 'Archie, our Beckham Estate Community Project Manager, has kindly said we can stop with him at Number 1 for the time being. What do you say?'

Flat Number 1 is not higher than the birds. It is

on the ground. But Archie is not a stranger, he is a friend. Mrs Hubert would not count Archie for my homework because Archie is old. But he is still my new green friend.

'Have you got any digestive biscuits?' I asked.

Everyone laughed, but I was not making a joke.

'Yes,' Archie said. 'I have digestives.'

'Then I would like to accept your invitation.'

Gran had her happy face on.

There was another loud explosion. I could hear screaming.

But before my world melted, Sasha my new amber friend held my hands in her hands. They were warm and soft.

The police from the van started walking in a line with their shields held out in front of them towards the riot.

Archie turned to Fox and said, 'We need to get out of this now.' He turned to Fox. 'Seeing that you can't get home to your flat either, may I extend my invitation to you and your daughter to come and shelter at my abode?'

Fox put his arm around Sasha, 'Hey, that's really good of you, thanks, man.'

We followed Archie to flat Number 1. A policeman saw us struggling to get through and walked next to us screaming at anyone who came too close to 'GET BACK'.

We reached Archie's flat and as I was wheeled through the door my mouth fell open. The room was filled with pictures from World War 2 and books and medals and an old parachute. In the corner of the living room was a piece of a Spitfire propeller.

Archie wanted to fly too.

8

Sasha

It was like stepping back into war times, like in that film *Hope and Glory*. I had never seen nothing like it in all my days. Old model planes hung from the ceiling. I hit my head on one of them. A bit of plane propeller stood in the corner, next to a piano and stuff! Stuff everywhere, boxes and boxes of stuff tipping out on to the floor, swirling round us. It was proper fantastic.

'Your flat is very messy, Archie,' said Willem.

'Give the man a chance, Willem, he's only just moved in,' said his gran.

My dad just stood there smiling, looking around him with his guitar in his hand.

'I am so very sorry, do sit down,' said Archie, pushing a battered old suitcase off a big armchair.

'Mrs Smith,' he said to Willem's gran, 'perhaps you would like to sit here.'

'Don't mind if I do,' she said.

Archie took her coat like a proper gentleman.

'Call me Gracie,' she said. 'I would like all of you to call me Gracie.'

'I shall call you Gran,' said Willem.

'She didn't mean you.' I laughed. See what I mean when I say that Willem takes things dead literal.

'All being well, I should have something really special to add to this collection soon,' said Archie.

'What? Go on, tell us, PLEASE,' I said.

Archie tapped the end of his nose and his eyes twinkled at me.

'It is time for Gran's tea and biscuits,' said Willem.

Archie wheeled Willem into the kitchen. I could hear cups clanking around. I pushed aside piles of clothes and Dad and I balanced on the end of the sofa. He still had his guitar in his hand. He put the other around my shoulder. I flinched where his arm touched the sore place, where my turquoise top was ripped underneath the jacket. My shoulder started to properly throb. But I never shook Dad's arm off, 'cause it's rare for him to hug me.

Outside, a window smashed. Someone screamed. Another siren sliced the air.

My gut flipped. Where was Finn? What had he done to Mrs Patel? The questions cut me. I had to try to reach him.

'Dad, can I have my phone?' He reached into his pocket and gave it to me, but it had run out of juice.

Gracie was looking at me with her beadies.

'I'd take that jacket off if I was you,' she said, 'now you're indoors.'

'No, it's all right,' I said, pulling Archie's jacket round me. 'I'm cold.'

But I wasn't. I just didn't want them all to see my ripped top.

Archie wheeled Willem back into the front room. Willem was balancing a tray of tea stuff with a big plate of digestives across his lap.

'We should all have sugar in our tea,' said Archie. 'I reckon we've all had a bit of a shock and it's the best thing for it.'

It was true what Archie said. The hot sweet tea made me feel like Sasha again. I suddenly had the munchies bad and grabbed two digestives like a proper pig.

Shouts and cusses from outside smacked my ears. I ran to the window to have a nosy. One of the T Crew boys was getting himself arrested. Archie shut the curtains. They were a deep red and a warm glow trickled around the room.

Willem was screwing up his face as he added milk to Gracie's tea slowly, slowly till he got it just right.

'Perfect, Willem,' said Gracie, munching her biscuits. Willem smiled like it was this major big achievement. My dad was looking up at the planes with his gob hanging open like a little kid, and Archie was sipping his tea, peeping over the top of the cup, with his twinkly eyes and his foot doing a little jig.

Slowly the warm glow from the curtains trickled into my belly. It was like being with a family, as if it was more than just me and Dad and it made me feel safe. I stretched my legs out in front of me – and my foot wacked something hard. It was an old wooden chest.

'Sorry, Archie,' I said.

'It's quite all right, my dear. Open it. Go on,' he said. 'I want you and Willem to see what's inside.' And he pushed Willem's wheelchair nearer to the chest.

It took my whole strength, with Willem's help,

to force it open. On the top, folded in old tissue paper, was a red dress. It looked like something straight from the nineteen-forties. I shook it out and held it to me. It was heavy and fell against my legs and smelled of lavender and cedar wood. It was stunning.

'This was my mother's. Her name was Rachel,' Archie said. 'I've not opened the chest for years, but I know she would want you to see her things. She wore that dress to dances. She loved to dance.'

I stood up and held it against me and swirled around. 'The colour suits you.' Gracie clapped.

'See what else is in there. I do not like dresses,' said Willem. Handing the red dress to Archie, I reached into the chest and pulled out two leather flying hats – the kind that have flappy ears.

'These were your mum's?' I asked.

'She was a pilot with the ATA – the Air Transport Auxiliary,' said Archie. 'My mother flew Spitfires in the war. Delivered them from the factories to the airfields, ready for the men to fly off to fight. She told me at night-time she danced with soldiers in the red dress, and in the daytime she danced with the clouds in the Spitfire.'

Willem and I looked at each other.

Imagine, I thought, flying a real aeroplane, not pretending like I do, but really up there dancing in the clouds. Willem reached out and put the flying hat on his head. I squeezed my head into the other one.

Archie reached for a camera on the shelf.

'Smile,' he said. I leaned over the back of Willem's wheelchair and put my arms around his shoulders. Willem held out his arm wings and Archie took a photo of us.

I lifted out of the chest Rachel's blue ATA uniform and her flying suit. At the bottom of the chest was a pair of black high-heeled shoes with an ankle strap and a beaded clutch bag. I opened it. Inside was a powder compact. A few grains of face powder lay in the bottom of the bag and there was a folded-up bit of faded yellow paper. I opened it slowly and proper delicately. It was a note.

An X FOR YOU TO KEEP
SAFE UNTIL I COME HOME.
Robert

'Who's Robert?' I asked, smoothing the creases in the note real careful.

'Flight Lieutenant Robert Howard Walker was her sweetheart,' said Archie. 'They first met when she was sent to ferry him from airfield to airfield on a special mission. She said it was love at first sight.'

'Oh that's proper romantic,' I said.

'In between flying Robert around, she would ferry Spitfires that needed repairing back to the factory,' continued Archie. 'She missed him dreadfully on the days she didn't see him. My mother would keep her fingers crossed every morning, when she was given her work chit with the flying instructions for the day, that she would be asked to fly to the airfield where Robert was stationed.'

'And was she?' I burst out.

'Sometimes she would just catch a glimpse of him across the airfield. He would leave love notes for her in secret places in the Spitfires for her to find. She said it was the most irresistible treasure hunt ever. Exactly twenty-one days after they first met, she delivered a Spitfire from the factory to the airfield where Robert was stationed. An air raid went off and they all had to rush to the shelter – they played cards to keep awake and talked through the night. The next day she had to fly a different Spitfire back to the factory for a repair and when she climbed in the cockpit she found this note. Robert had left it for her. That was the last note she got. He didn't come home. He was shot down in his Hurricane plane.'

I had to quickly banish a tear. I'm telling you I'm not usually that soppy. I put my head down quick so no one could see and kept proper busy, folding up the note and putting it back where it belonged in Rachel's bag.

'Archie, was Flight Lieutenant Robert Howard Walker your father?' asked Willem.

'No,' said Archie. 'My father was called Stanley, she met him after the war had finished. He was a very serious man and did not like to dance.'

I reached into the bottom of the chest and felt the corner of a book. I pulled it out. It was a photo album. I opened it and there staring back at me was Rachel. I SWEAR MY HEART STOPPED, 'cause she had dark eyes like me, but hers were dancing, and she had black hair like me, but hers was blowing in the wind. She was standing on the wing of a beautiful Spitfire plane, one arm reaching towards the sky, the propeller sticking out behind her, ready for take off. A parachute was slung over her shoulder. She looked so free and strong and everything I wanted to be. Everything I tried to be but wasn't. If Finn Mason said 'run' to Rachel, she wouldn't run, she would stand and do what she wanted to do – what she believed. I felt pure shame.

Archie looked at me, like he knew what I was thinking. He took the photo out of the album and handed it to me.

'My mother found it hard with all those male pilots – some of them believed women shouldn't fly and gave her a tough time, but she could fly as well as any of them. What you did today, sticking up for Willem, took guts and I want you to have this.'

'Truth?' I said, feeling proper astonished.

'Truth,' said Archie, smiling. 'It's yours, keep it.'

I didn't feel brave. I just felt I'd messed up. Rachel the Spitfire pilot was a proper inspirational woman; thinking about her made a fire burn in my belly.

'Where's your bathroom, Archie?' I asked.

He nodded down the corridor.

I shut the bathroom door behind me and put the

photo on a shelf. Rachel stared back at me. I looked in the mirror and eased Archie's jacket off my shoulder. Through the ripped top I could see that it was red and starting to bruise.

A knock startled me. The bathroom door opened. Gracie stepped in and closed the door behind her.

'I thought so,' she said. 'I knew you were hiding something.' She was carrying Rachel's red dress and black strappy shoes.

'Let's get this off you.' She helped me lift the turquoise top over my head. 'We'll soon get that mended.' She reached into her bag and brought out some ointment and gently rubbed it into my shoulder. It burned.

'Archie said you could wear this dress if you want – said it was made for dancing, not for being locked in a trunk.'

I wriggled out of my jeans. Gracie lifted the dress over my head. It rippled down over my body like a silk stream. It was a little baggy over my bumps and shoulders. Gracie brought safety pins out of her handbag and carefully pinned it till it fitted me like a glove.

'Would you like me to do your hair and make-up

to go with it?'

I nodded 'cause I couldn't speak.

Gracie started pinning and rolling my hair and then reached into her bag and took out a red lipstick and put it on me. She took out a brown pencil and filled in my eyebrows.

'Don't you look the part? All you need now is seams down the back of your legs. The women never had tights because of rations so they used to draw 'em on.'

'Let's do it, Gracie,' I said. 'The drawing-seams-on-legs scene is my favourite bit in that *Hope and Glory* film.'

She got out an eye pencil and closed the toilet seat. 'Stand on it. I'm too old to bend down.'

It tickled, and me and Gracie clutched on to each other laughing 'cause I kept wobbling and nearly falling off the toilet. I climbed down and stepped into the black shoes and fastened the ankle straps. They were a bit tight but I DIDN'T CARE.

I looked in the mirror and it was like Rachel stared back.

I felt fire in my belly like I COULD DO ANYTHING.

I could hear my dad playing guitar riffs, then the

piano joined in and it sounded like proper nineteen-forties' big band music. Living with a musician like my dad means you don't grow up only knowing about hip hop! My toes started tapping and before I knew it Gracie and I were dancing down the hall and into the front room.

Archie stopped playing for a millisecond when he saw me, then his voice cracked as he said, 'Rachel, my old mum, would have so loved to have seen you dancing in her red dress.'

'You look like a film star,' shouted Dad above the music.

Willem was playing the drums on the tea tray. He was out of time but drumming to his own rhythm. I grabbed his hands and we did the wheelchair jive, 'cause I can be proper inventive when I want to be.

Archie was pure talent on the piano. The music zinged and we were all jumping and jiving. Gracie showed me some jitterbug and jive steps, and even though the sirens and the sound of breaking glass were just outside, I didn't care.

I danced Finn right out of my brain and my heart. I danced for Rachel. I danced for Robert, who got shot down and never got to kiss Rachel. Then over the beat

came the sound of a dog barking. It was Buster. I ran
to the door and opened it.

Finn fell, cut and bleeding, through the door.

9

Sasha

Everything moved in slow motion as Finn crumpled in a heap at my feet. The music stopped and there was this whimpering noise and I realized it was me saying 'NO, NO, NOOO,' inside my head, and there was this howling and Buster was standing over Finn's body, dog-crying.

'FINN!' I screamed. 'FINN, CAN YOU HEAR ME?'

He turned his head slowly, slowly, and held out his hand towards me. I held it tight, but blood seeped in between my fingers. I leaned forward and I know I had made a vow to myself that I wouldn't kiss Finn yet, but I wanted to make him better, so I leaned down and gave him a tiny quick kiss on the lips – not a snog or anything, what with him being wounded and my dad being in the room. Just a little gentle kiss to make him not hurt. But as I raised my head, I turned and Willem was jerking about in his chair, trying to jump. My gut flipped and I suddenly didn't want to kiss Finn, I wanted to punch him.

'WILLEM, STOP!' I screamed. 'HE CAN'T MAKE YOU JUMP. HE CAN'T HURT YOU. LOOK AT HIM.' I felt a pair of arms around me and my dad was lifting me off the floor. He grabbed hold of Buster's trailing lead and led us both to the armchair.

'Give them some room, Sash,' he said. Gracie had some flannels and a bowl of steaming water and Archie had a battered old green first aid tin.

I put my arms around Buster and watched as Archie slowly moved Finn's legs and arms – I suppose to check if they were broken.

Finn let out a dull moan.

Gracie kneeled down on her old knees and started to wash his cuts and bruises and get the mud out of his blond curls. Finn had his eyes tight shut and bit his lip, flinching. Gracie eased his T-shirt off his mashed-up body, but it stuck to him 'cause of the dried blood. It looked like he had been kicked in the stomach again and again.

Finn turned his head to look at me and tried

to say something.

'What, Finn?' I said.

'Buster dragged me here,' he whispered. 'I couldn't hardly walk but Buster – he kept dragging me along, tugging at his lead.'

'He must've followed your trail, Sasha,' said Gracie.

'Clever Buster,' I said. 'Good boy.' And he licked my cheek. I unhooked his lead and gave him the last digestive biscuit.

Glass shattered outside. The riot was exploding. Police screamed at youths and youths screamed back. Dogs barked and sirens squealed. My head banged. Archie looked through the curtains.

'I reckon we are all holed up here for the night – best make the most of it.'

He disappeared and came back with quilts and sheets and pillows.

'Gracie,' he said. 'I would like you to take my bed, in the other room.'

'Sasha can come in with me,' said Gracie.

Archie and Dad lifted Finn on to the sofa and helped Willem hobble into the armchair, folding his wheelchair in the corner. Finn gazed up at the model planes hanging from the ceiling and smiled for the first time. Archie found a stool for Willem's fractured foot to rest on, and my dad made beds on the floor for him and Archie.

'All sorted,' I said, looking round. 'It's like a proper camp.'

'But, Archie, we have to eat supper before we go to bed,' said Willem.

'Sausages and mash do you?' said Archie.

I followed Gracie and Archie into the kitchen and washed Finn's blood off my hands. Before I knew it they had me peeling potatoes and chopping onions. I kept peeping through the kitchen door at Finn, but he was still lying there with his eyes closed.

'Concentrate on what you're doing,' said Gracie. 'He'll mend.'

Willem cracks me up, he had his sausage and mash on separate plates. It was proper cosy sitting down to our feast in our camp.

I woke to the sound of Gracie snoring and for a second my brain blanked – then it kicked into action jolt by jolt and I remembered everything.

Riots. Archie. Running out of school. Willem. It was Saturday, so at least I didn't have to face Mrs

Hubert till Monday. Finn! I had to know what he did to the Patel's shop – how much trouble was he in?

Gracie did an extra-loud snort and turned over, pulling all of the quilt over her. I shuffled out of bed and crept slowly, slowly out and into the front room. I nearly fell over my dad and landed with a bump against the sofa. Buster was curled up on the floor and growled in his sleep. Finn opened his eyes.

'Shh,' I whispered. 'I want words with you. Kitchen, now. Can you make it?'

He nodded. As I helped him up, Buster woke and scrambled on to the sofa, burying under Finn's covers. Finn limped in front of me to the kitchen.

I shut the door and put on the light. Finn's mashed-up body was covered by a yellow T-shirt Archie had given him. I was wearing Archie's huge old man's shirt that he had given me to sleep in. I pulled it down over my legs.

'Right,' I said. 'NO LIES. How could you steal from Mrs Patel? Mrs Patel who's known you for like for ever and has always, always given us extra sweets. How could you, Finn?'

'Sasha, know the facts before you go shouting your mouth off,' said Finn. 'All right, I got carried away. I was with the Beckham Boyz and some of the T Crew and they was breaking windows and looting the betting shop, but Buster was scared and howling and pulling at me, making a show of me, so I couldn't join in.'

'That dog's got more brains than you,' I hissed.

'Are you going to let me tell you what happened or what?'

'Go on then,' I said, 'but I'm serious – no lies.'

'I grabbed Buster's lead to take him back home,' said Finn, 'and I started walking across the yard but I heard this scream, and I just knew it was Mrs Patel, 'cause of that time I showed her my pet rat, Spud, when I was in juniors. I recognized the scream, right, and I turned round and I ran back to the shops and they had started looting the newsagent. They was robbing all of the Patels' stuff, and they had locked Mr Patel in the back office. I ran in and Mrs Patel looked right at me.

'"Finn,"' she said, "not you," and she had, like, this fear in her eyes, 'cause she thought I was going to loot her stuff. That look, it made me feel like I had a blade in my gut. So I grabbed a box of crisps and ran up her stairs to the flat, 'cause I thought their stuff would be safer up there, but she followed me, screaming.

'"Not my house. Get out of my house," and she thought I was going to rob her, and the way she looked at me made the blade in my gut slash deeper, so I said, "Mrs Patel, I am trying to save your crisps – where shall I hide 'em?"

'Only Richie Lane heard me, 'cause he'd followed me up the stairs, and he told the gang elders and they dragged me outside and gave me a kicking. You've got to believe me, Sash.'

My eyes searched his bruised face and I wanted to believe him, I really did, but doubt kicked me.

'I believe you,' said a voice behind me.

I turned. It was Willem, standing on one leg in the doorway. Finn just stared at him with his mouth open like a muppet.

'Can I have a glass of water please?' said Willem.

I filled a glass from the sink and gave it to Willem. He was still dressed in his school uniform from yesterday. He downed the water in one. A bird sang outside. I pulled the blind up. Daylight was coming.

There was a knock at the front door.

'Open up. It's the police,' shouted a voice.

10

WILLEM

Bang, bang, bang. 'Open up. It's the police,' shouted the angry voice.

'Finn Mason, we know you're in there.' Bang, bang, bang. 'You were seen coming in.'

My fingers started to jiggle, so I snatched my Spitfire from my pocket. Buster was barking.

Finn grabbed Sasha's arm. 'You gotta believe me, Sash.'

I heard Archie open the door and then mumbling voices.

'Finn,' called Archie. 'Finn, where are you?'

Finn heaved himself on to the sink draining board and tried to force open the kitchen window, but it was locked.

'If you ain't done nothing, why are you trying

to run?' said Sasha.

''Cause they ain't going to believe me, are they?' said Finn.

'My gran says *you've got to stand your ground and face what's coming*,' I said.

'Willem's right. You've gotta face it,' said Sasha and she pulled Finn off the top of the sink by the back of his yellow T-shirt and stretched the other arm out to me. Finn had his scared face on. I held on to her and hobbled through to the front room.

2 policemen, one with black stubbly hair and the other tall with a red nose, stood in the front room either side of Archie. They had left the front door open. The one with the black stubbly hair was looking around at the pictures from World War 2, and the books and medals and old parachute and the piece of Spitfire propeller. The one with the red nose was staring at Fox, who was sitting on the sofa rubbing his eyes. His hair was sticking up more than usual. I don't think people who used to be rock stars ever comb their hair.

'Ah, Finn Mason,' said the one with the red nose when he spotted Finn. 'We meet again. We'd like you to come down to the station for a little chat.'

'It weren't me,' said Finn.

'It's always you,' said the one with black stubbly hair. 'Now if you would like to come with us . . .'

'Officers, please, could we just cool it? This boy's not fit to go anywhere,' said Fox.

'Finn hasn't had his breakfast yet,' I said.

My gran marched in, dressed and ready for the day, carting her big black handbag and Sasha's torn turquoise top.

'Have you seen the state of him?' said Gran to the policemen, and she lifted up Finn's T-shirt. Yellow, black and green bruises were forming round the grazes and cuts.

There was a knock at the open front door.

'Hello,' called a voice. 'Got a voice message from someone called Archie that my son is here. Umm – I've brought him a change of clothes.'

'Come in,' shouted Archie, and Trish, who is Finn's mum, came through the door carrying a bag. She was wearing pink trainers. She had a bruise on her arm. She stopped when she saw the policemen.

'What's he been up to?' said Trish.

'It weren't me, Mum,' said Finn.

'It's always you,' said Trish.

'Let the boy speak,' said Gran.

Finn told the policemen the truths of Mrs Patel and the crisps and being dragged outside by the elders of the gang and beaten up.

'They left me by the bins,' said Finn. 'I was knocked out, so I couldn't have done any rioting, see? My dog Buster, he was jumping up at them, growling when they was punching me. When I woke up, he was lying on me, licking my face. I managed to drag myself up and Buster started pulling me towards this flat, followed Sasha's trail, so here I am.'

'Good story,' said the policeman with the red nose.

'Very inventive,' said the policeman with the black stubbly hair. 'If you would just like to come with us – and if you could accompany him, Mrs Mason,' he said to Trish.

Then there was jostling and shouting. Finn was being taken out through the door. My Spitfire propeller was spinning fast and Trish was crying.

'STOP, STOP!' I shouted in my loudest voice. 'IT IS NOT A STORY. FINN IS TELLING THE TRUTH,' I said. 'I CAN PROVE IT.'

The policemen stopped in their tracks and turned to face me. Finn stared at me with his mouth wide open.

'Very commendable, sticking up for your friend,' said the policeman with the red nose.

'Finn is not my friend,' I said. 'I do not like him. I would be happy if you locked him up. I would not have to jump off things.'

'You're dead,' mouthed Finn. My body shook, but I ignored him.

'Where is the T-shirt Finn wore yesterday?' I asked.

'I put it in the laundry basket,' said Gran. 'It needs a good soak.'

'Sasha, please could you fetch it?' I said.

Sasha stared at me, then marched off to the bathroom. I don't think she believed that Finn had not been in the riot. She brought back Finn's bloodstained T-shirt. I picked up Finn's jeans that were hanging over the back of the sofa and hobbled towards the policeman with the red nose.

'If you look at these, officer, there is dog hair woven through the fabric, which indicates my friend Buster here had been lying on Finn for a considerable length of time. Hold your right palm out, Finn,' I said.

Finn did. 'There is a red line across it where Buster was pulling on the lead. This indicates that Buster had been pulling for some time. If Finn was stealing trainers and sweets he would not have this line on his hand. Finn fell through this door at 8.15 p.m., and was here all night when the other boys were rioting outside. I have a very fine-tuned sense of smell and I detected the faint smell of the bins when he first fell through the door. Lastly, my gran had difficulty taking this T-shirt off Finn, as the blood had dried and stuck the T-shirt to his body, which indicated he had been lying unconscious for a while.'

No one spoke. The sound of silence crackled in my ears. This always happens to me when people do not use words. Everyone was looking at me. I spun the Spitfire propeller faster and faster.

The policeman with the red nose cleared his throat. 'Well, ummph, you would make a good detective, son.'

'I am not your son,' I said. 'I do not want to be a detective. I would not like to arrest strangers.

I want to fly when I am grown up.'

'We will say our goodbyes,' said the 2 policemen.

The policeman with the black stubbly hair pointed his finger at Finn. 'You stay out of trouble,' he said. 'We've got enough on our hands. You were lucky he was here.' He pointed at me.

My gran says it's rude to point.

The policeman with the red nose said, 'Fox, can I just say when my wife was a teenager she was Zebra Blue's biggest fan, plays your old tracks all the time especially "You Got Me Bad". We danced to it at our wedding.'

The policeman with the black stubbly hair glared at him.

'Sorry, sir,' said the policeman with the red nose and the 2 policemen left.

Finn hobbled over to me and held out his fist. I held out my clenched fist to his and they touched. No one has ever done that to me before.

'Cheers, Willem,' he said.

Could this mean that Finn wants to be my friend and will not make me jump off things?

'Hey, well done, Willem, man,' said Fox.

Finn held his arms out to Sasha. 'See, told you.'

95

But she turned her back on him and walked over to the Spitfire propeller and put out her hands to touch it.

Trish gave me a quick kiss on the cheek before I could move away. 'Thank you from the bottom of my heart,' she said. She had black circles under her eyes.

'Time for breakfast,' said Archie. 'You will join us, won't you?' he said to Trish.

'No, thanks, I'd best get back to his dad. He won't be happy if he doesn't get his bacon and eggs. Thanks for all you've done for Finn. All of you – you're good people.' Her voice cracked, which is a sign that happiness and sadness had got mixed up. 'You behave, Finn. I MEAN IT.'

She kissed Sasha and Finn goodbye and left.

Archie made us all tea and toast. He switched on the television and there was Gran on the news, waving her handbag, shouting at the rioters. The news man called her 'a pillar of the community'.

'Gran, you are famous like Fox,' I said. Everyone laughed, but I was not making a joke. Gran was mending Sasha's top as she watched the television. She had her happy face on.

Then the television showed pictures of the police battering down doors and dragging people out with handcuffs on in streets and estates all over London. The news reached the Beckham Estate and the battering down of the doors on the television echoed the battering down of doors outside, and I realized they were filming live. It was happening now and I hobbled across the room to the front door. Everyone followed me and we went outside.

11

WILLEM

There was a scream. TJ's mum, Aunty Lou, came running through her front door, which is Number 5 Beckham Estate. 2 policemen had TJ in handcuffs. He was being arrested.

It was very messy outside.

'Sasha, Finn, get dressed now,' said Gran. 'You can't run around outside in your night things. It's not decent.' Sasha rolled her eyes. Finn held his hand out to Sasha, but she pushed past him and ran back into Archie's flat. Finn ran after her. I do not think they are friends any more.

'Gran,' I said, 'I am in my school uniform. Today is not a school day. I need my Saturday clothes.'

Aunty Lou was still screaming.

'Not now, Willem,' said Gran, 'please, I can't

get your Saturday clothes now.'

The 2 policemen were putting TJ into the back of a police car. He was crying. My brain tangled. My fingers jiggled. Archie got my wheelchair and helped me into it. Gran pushed me across the broken glass and ash and litter towards Number 5 Beckham Estate, which was Aunty Lou's flat. Buster jumped on my knees for the ride.

Gran took Aunty Lou's mobile from her jiggling fingers and phoned TJ's big sister, Alisha. She told her to get herself to the police station as TJ needed an adult present when he was questioned.

Sasha came running towards the car; Finn was behind her, pulling on his hoodie as he ran. Finn punched his fist in the air and thumped 3 of the fingers of his right hand into the palm of his left. This is their Beckham Street Boyz gang sign. They think their sign is top secret but I have decoded it. I see them do it under desks, in the playground, and in the darkest corners of our estate. As the police car drove off, TJ looked through the window and punched his fist in the air, giving the sign back to Finn.

'You!' screamed Aunty Lou at Finn. 'It's always

you when there's trouble. Why don't you leave my son alone?'

Finn stumbled backwards into my wheelchair. Gran put her hand on his shoulder.

'Aunty Lou,' said Sasha, 'you know I respect you more than the sky is blue, and I would never ever tell you a blatant lie, but this time for once it weren't Finn. TJ robbed the TV from the bookies all by himself. I saw him. We all saw him. He don't need much encouragement to be a muppet.'

Aunty Lou had tears leaking from her eyes.

'You children, when will you ever learn?'

Finn smiled at Sasha, but she turned her back on him. They are still not friends.

Bang! Bang! Bang! Doors forced open, boys in handcuffs being put in the back of police vans and cars. Dogs barking. Screams. Crying. My brain tangled. I saw Laurence being dragged into the back of a police van shouting and kicking. The van drove off. Buster jumped off my knees and ran after it, barking. My fingers jiggled. I closed my eyes. I flew up into the sky and spun round a rain cloud. A blackbird's wing brushed my nose. Then I felt a hand on mine and

I opened my eyes and it was Finn.

He was squatting in front of my wheelchair, staring straight at me. He screwed up his nose. His 7 freckles disappeared.

'Willem, it's all right. Don't stress.' I saw that Finn's brain was tangled and his fingers were jiggling. He had no friends. Sasha did not want to be his friend any more. All his other friends were being taken by the police. I had 1 amber friend (Sasha) and 3 green friends (Buster and Bernie from the Burger Bar and Archie). I also had Gran – but she is a relative so that doesn't count.

Finn might need another friend. Me. I smiled at him and held my fist out. He touched it with his shaking fist.

'You had best get out of Lou's sight. Go and see if Archie needs a hand,' Gran said to Finn.

Finn nodded his head. 'I'll go and find Buster.'

'Let's get you a cuppa tea,' said Gran and put her arm around Aunty Lou.

Sasha wheeled me into Number 5 after them.

A place for everything and everything in its place, Aunty Lou always said. But everything was not in its place. The police had turned her front room upside down looking for stolen goods. Ornaments and books and photographs lay topsy-turvy. Aunty Lou had 14 figurines of the Virgin Mary and 5 Baby Jesuses. 1 of the Baby Jesuses wore a blue dress and looked a bit cross. She had 3 Angel Gabriels with magnificent wings. Gran says when kind people smile upon you it is the angels sending blessings from heaven. Sasha is my angel.

'I will never get them back how they were,' said Aunty Lou, looking round her.

'I will do it,' I said, 'I remember exactly where everything was.' I started to put things back one by one in their correct place. My fingers stopped jiggling. My brain untangled even though I was not in my Saturday clothes.

There was a photograph of TJ and me, feeding the ducks in the park when we were 6, before he made me jump off things.

I could hear the sound of chopping. Aunty Lou always chops carrots when she is angry. She says it makes her feel better, but taking things out on vegetables does not solve problems.

Sasha left me alone to go into the kitchen. I held a glass Angel Gabriel that Aunty Lou had bought in

Venice up to the sunlight coming through the window. As I turned the angel, red, blues and indigos flew around the room, caused by refraction as the different colours that make white light travelled through the glass at different speeds and angles. White light is made up of red, orange, yellow, green, blue, indigo and violet. I learned this in Science, which is my 2nd favourite subject after Maths.

As the colours spun around the room, I shut my eyes and I was flying with them faster and faster. The chopping got louder and louder. Food smells tickled my nose.

'Willem . . . Willem . . .' Sasha was calling me. I bumped back down into my wheelchair. Aunty Lou, Gran and Sasha were in the front room, looking round them.

'You've done a good job, Willem. Thank you,' said Aunty Lou. 'Only you could restore order from such chaos.'

'I like tidying,' I said. 'I want to tidy the estate now.'

Sasha laughed, but I was not making a joke. Tidying makes me feel calm.

'Why not?' said Aunty Lou, putting her hand on my head which I do not like, so I counted to 10.

'Yes, why not indeed,' shouted Gran. 'Come on. Willem, you and Sasha see if you can round up some volunteers. I'll do teas and coffees for the helpers.'

'I've got some curry goat and rice cooking,' said Aunty Lou, wiggling her hips. 'We'll lay on a spread.'

'Come on,' said Sasha, as she grabbed my wheelchair and pushed me outside.

I felt happy. I had put order back into Aunty Lou's front room and now I wanted to put order back into the Beckham Estate, my home. It was what I wanted more than anything in the whole world.

It was then that I saw the megaphone lying in a puddle. The fireman must have dropped it in the riot. I reached out for it and grabbed it.

Sasha ran round and round the courtyard, pushing me past the burned-out cars and over the ash and dirt.

'Bring your mops, bring your buckets, bring your brooms. Bring food. We are going to make the Beckham Estate our home again,' I shouted through the megaphone.

Round and round we went.

Doors opened. People peeped out at us. Archie, Finn and Fox stood in the doorway of Number 1, waving at us, smiling. Buster ran out and crashed into the wheelchair.

Then Bernie came round the corner with a stack of tables from Bernie's Burger Bar and set them in a row. Aunty Lou and Gran brought out a huge pot of curry goat and a pot of rice and Mrs Patel brought a big plate of samosas and Bernie brought the burgers. The food was all laid on the tables.

Then they started to come in 1s and 2s and 3s. People coming down the stairs and out of the lift and walking across the courtyard towards me and Sasha. People carrying brooms and mops and buckets and plates of jollof rice and jerk chicken and noodles and muufo bread and hvorost and risotto and chips and plates of sandwiches. Food for everyone to share. More and more people came. The chattering sounds of all the languages jammed in my ears but my brain did not tangle. Sasha handed me a bin bag. My fingers did not jiggle. The smells of the heavenly food that people were putting on Bernie's tables itched my nose. I would need a lot of plates to taste it all.

Archie came out and hopped and skipped around, organizing everyone into teams. We picked up our brooms and we started to sweep.

12

Sasha

We were a lean mean sweeping machine. Willem had a broom in each hand and I was pushing his wheelchair up and down. Buster was sitting on Willem's knees, barking, then jumping off and trying to bite the broom, and we were laughing ourselves silly.

But inside I wasn't laughing. Inside I was edgy. As we went up and down and round and round, I searched for Finn, my mind racing. Finn had held out his hand to me, but I'd refused it. Then he'd smiled at me, after I'd stuck up for him when Aunty Lou went mental. But again I'd turned my back on him. Why had I done that? Why, why, why? Where was he? Now that I'd had my head space, it was time to make up with him. But he'd vanished. Typical!

I knew that without a doubt Willem's evidence

proved that Finn did not loot Mrs Patel's shop, and I'm soooo relieved 'cause I would never have forgiven him. I promise you, I would never have spoken to him again. Not ever.

My eyes were piercing the crowd for Finn till I felt dizzy. Women everywhere were covering their hair with scarves tied in turbans to keep the dust off. It looked like the blitz scenes in *Hope and Glory*. Gracie grabbed me and tied a blue scarf round my hair.

'That'll do you, girl,' she said.

'Have you seen, Finn?' I asked her.

'No, now you come to mention it.'

'Come on, Willem,' I said and the lean mean sweeping machine moved faster and faster, searching for Finn. We spun round the corner at top speed straight into the path of my teacher, Mrs Hubert, who was marching along with a big plate of sandwiches in one hand and a dustpan and brush in the other. I slammed the brakes on Willem's wheelchair and dived behind it just in time.

I curled up really small. I should have guessed she'd come 'cause she's proper community-minded, is Mrs Hubert. It seemed like a million years ago, not yesterday, when I ran out of her class to go to the hospital. I was on my last chance. She would give me detention for for ever if she saw me. I would still be in school when I was older than Gracie. I peeped round the side of the chair. Mr Richardson the headteacher and Mr Patricks the caretaker were behind her. Probably just come to have a nosy after the riots. I watched as Archie went over to them.

'Sasha, why are you hiding behind my wheelchair?' said Willem, in a proper loud voice.

'Shh,' I said, but it was too late.

'Sasha Barton, there must be something very interesting on the ground. Are you still looking for your earring?'

She is sooo sarky.

I stood up.

'SASHA, YOU HAVE HAD YOUR LAST CHANCE. YOU, YOUNG LADY, ARE IN DEEP TROUBLE, RUNNING OUT OF SCHOOL LIKE THAT.'

'Mrs Hubert,' said Willem, 'Sasha ran out of school to help me.'

'Be quiet, Willem,' spat Mrs Hubert, which I thought was pure rudeness.

'You can't tell me off, Mrs Hubert. It is Saturday,' said Willem.

109

Before I could help it, this proper snorty laugh escaped from my gob and I pretended I WAS COUGHING.

Mrs Hubert wasn't having any of it. 'Oh, so you think it's funny, do you? Let's see how funny you find it when you are standing in Mr Richardson's office.'

'Please, Mrs Hubert,' I begged. 'PLEEEEASE – it was an emergency.'

At that moment Mr Richardson marches up and sticks his beak in. 'Sasha Barton – MY OFFICE, MONDAY.'

I felt sick to my gut.

'Mr Richardson,' said Willem, 'Sasha is very brave. She protected me from the rioters and got me back to my gran, so I would not have to live with strangers. You should give her a merit mark.'

'MONDAY,' said Mr Richardson and stormed off.

'He does not practise good listening skills,' said Willem.

'Sasha, you can start to make amends by working really hard today in the community clear-up,' said Mrs Hubert. 'I will be watching you.' She grabbed hold of one of Willem's brooms and shoved it in my hand, and marched off to squeeze her plate of smelly fish paste sandwiches next to the curry goat.

'But Mrs Hubert,' Willem shouted after her, 'even though I think she would rather have been with Finn, Sasha stayed with me. You told me to make two friends. Sasha is my first friend. I have done half of my homework.'

But Mrs Hubert ignored Willem.

I flung my arms around Willem and kissed him on the cheek, but he shied away from me. It stung for a second, but I told myself that Willem can't help his ways. I proper love that boy for trying to stick up for me.

'I wouldn't have rather been with Finn,' I told him. 'Being with you was just fine, thank you very much.'

'Is that a truth?' said Willem.

'It's an honest truth,' I said.

He gave me a lovely smile that cut my heart, 'cause Willem has spent so much time on his own and I hate thinking about that. I should have reached out to him way before now, 'cause his mum ran off and left him too and I know what that's like. I have lost too many friendship days with Willem, but from now on I am grabbing hold of them with a tight fist. No more time shall slip through my fingers.

'You will have to stand your ground and face what's coming, like my gran always says,' said Willem.

'I know I will, Willem,' I said, feeling the fear.

Mrs Hubert's beadies were on me, so I parked the lean mean sweeping machine behind the table where Gracie was making teas and coffees so that Willem could help, 'cause he likes making tea, does Willem. Buster stayed there 'cause of the plates of digestives. I robbed one and sneaked it to him when Gracie wasn't looking.

Mrs Hubert was still shooting evils at me, so I started to sweep, while still searching for Finn. I swept till my arms were aching and I couldn't sweep no more.

I leaned on my broom for a breather.

The chatter of different tongues swam around me. Archie was showing a couple of oldies, who don't speak good English, what to do. Even though they don't get Archie's words, they get his twinkly eyes and kind ways. That is a gift. A touch of lightness tickled my heart as magic man Archie disappeared up the road with a hop and a skip and a jig till he was a little ziggy spot.

Trish swept by me, her pink trainers all dusty. She

was sweeping funny, as if her arm was hurting.

'You seen Finn?' I yelled. She shook her head.

I just had to find him before our fall-out got too big to mend.

I heard a commotion behind me. I turned round. The press and TV cameras were here taking pictures of Gracie making the tea and coffee. Then one of them, a tall, lanky man with spiky hair who looked like a bog brush, recognized Dad.

'Aren't you that Fox out of Zebra Blue?' he shouted. He pushed past Willem and knocked his wheelchair so hard it wobbled.

'Oi! Watch where you're going,' I yelled.

He didn't even care, 'cause all he wanted was to take a picture of Dad and Gracie with their arms round each other, holding brooms. Dad had that smile of his plastered across his face, a mixture of embarrassed and pleased, reliving the old days.

Then the rest of the press swarmed round like wasps shouting, 'Fox, look this way . . . Fox, what is your opinion of the youth of today?'

'Look this way, Fox,' they kept shouting.

Willem had his hands over his ears and his eyes were shut. His fingers were doing that shaking thing.

I dropped my broom and ran over to him. I pushed his wheelchair far away from the cameras.

'Willem,' I said, 'Willem, look at me,' but he had gone into his own world. I hoped it was a nice world.

However edgy my gut felt, looking for Finn would just have to wait. I couldn't leave Willem. I sang 'Maisy's Rain' to him with lullaby calmness, till he stopped shaking and came back to me. I had a proper good idea to get him away from this madness.

'Willem, I am going to take you to the Patels'. We can help tidy the shop. Would you like that?'

He put out his hand and brushed my cheek like a feather.

'I think we should take them some food, Willem.'

He nodded.

I ran back to the table and shoved my way through the press, giving old bog-brush head an extra-big push. I loaded one of Aunty Lou's trays with teas and coffees, two bowls of curry goat and rice, and some cakes. I carried it round the back of the press scrum and made it back to Willem. He balanced the tray across the wheelchair arms and I pushed him, careful, careful, across the courtyard and round the corner to the shops.

We passed the bins where Mr Patricks, our school caretaker, was bossing everyone about, telling 'em where to put the rubbish, like at school. He nodded over to us.

We reached the Patels'. I opened the broken door with my bum and pulled Willem in backwards. There in the middle of the mashed-up shop was Finn, sitting on a stool with no T-shirt on.

'Hi, Finn,' I said, flicking my hair back and smiling my special smile.

'All right, Willem,' he said, totally blanking me.

Willem smiled like all his Christmases had come at once.

Finn's blond curls were falling across his eyes. My heart was busting. I know he can be a nutter. I know he does my head in, but when someone has been in your life for that long, they are part of you, even if you don't always like 'em. But suppose he didn't want to know me. Suppose he never talks to me again. My gut punched the floor.

Mrs Patel was smoothing yellow ointment on his cuts and bruises. It smelled like the wild flowers that tickle your nose in the morning, when you squeeze through the gap in the fence, behind the girls' changing rooms, if you take the forbidden shortcut to school.

After a proper awkward pause I said, 'Mrs Patel, I've brought some food for you and Mr Patel. We've come to help.'

'Ah, Sasha, how very kind,' she said. 'I am so sorry; I did try to tell you about Finn. That at first I thought he was up to no good but that I was mistaken – he was actually trying to help. But my words had quite gone, with all the ruckus.'

Guilt smacked me again.

'Finn, I'm sor—' I swallowed, 'cause saying sorry don't come that easy to me. 'I'm sorry, all right. I should never have doubted your words,' I whispered. 'But you can't blame me really, can you, 'cause of . . .'

And I never finished that sentence obviously 'cause of Mrs Patel's ears flapping, but we both knew I meant all the stuff he's robbed from school. 'Cause Finn thinks school stuff is public property or something.

Finn wouldn't look at me and the room was filled with a prickly vibe.

I just stood there, not knowing what to do next. Then, after what seemed like years, Finn suddenly laughed and stretched out his arm and pulled me to him. He pulled off my blue scarf turban then tweaked the end of my nose and winked at me.

'It's all right, Sash,' he said, and he gave me that look, that look of his that makes my knees go funny.

'Put Sasha down, Finn,' said Mrs Patel. 'She will get ointment all over her lovely turquoise top.'

My heart danced. I looked at Willem. His hands were doing that shaking thing.

A note from Willem

I tried to stop my hand jiggling. It was good that Sasha and Finn were now friends. It was very, very good that Finn was my new amber friend (proceed with caution), which meant I had done my homework and Mrs Hubert would be very pleased. But we had come to do tidying, not cuddling.

A lorry pulled up outside. A man opened the back of the van. It was full of crisps and sweets to replace the ones that had been looted by the rioters. I wanted to put them on the shelves to calm my mind.

'Look,' shouted Sasha. 'It's Gracie.'

I looked at where she was pointing. Today's newspapers had already arrived.

There was a picture of my gran on a lot of the front pages. It was taken yesterday when she had shouted at the rioters.

Pensioner Takes on Riot Yobs with Handbag

Pensioner Gracie Smith, who lives with her grandson Willem on the Beckham Estate, North West London, was one of the many hundreds of people forced to leave their homes due to yesterday's riots. Brave Mrs Smith turned and faced the rioters, waving her handbag in the air, naming them 'daft lads' and calling on them to stop the racket and to think about what they were doing. The television news named Mrs Smith a pillar of the community.

When asked to comment, Mrs Smith said, 'These young people have no direction in life. As the saying goes, "the devil makes work for idle hands". I understand that we have a new Community Project Manager on the estate. I will be interested to see what plans he has.

'And another thing. When are the council going to mend the lift? It's a disgrace!'

My gran was famous. I wondered if she would be asked to go on *I'm A Celebrity – Get Me Out of Here!* My gran would not like to eat bugs. She likes to eat digestive biscuits. Sasha pulled one of the newspapers from under the string that tied them and put it on my lap. My gran's face looked angry. I stroked her paper cheek.

Mr Patel started carrying boxes through to the stockroom. But Sasha stopped him and made the Patels sit down and eat the curry goat and rice. I poured the Patels some tea.

'Mr and Mrs Patel,' I asked, 'please can we put your crisps and chocolates on the shelves in the correct order? I remember where everything goes. We will make your shop tidy.'

'That would be most kind, Willem,' said Mrs Patel, sipping my tea. She smiled. I had made her happy. Mr Patel nodded, his mouth was full of curry goat and he could not speak, as it is rude to talk with your mouth full.

Then I instructed Sasha where to put all the different flavoured crisps, starting with salt and vinegar and ending with cheese and onion.

I felt brave as there was nothing in the shop

for Finn to make me jump off, so I told Finn where to put the Mars bars. It is usually Finn who tells *me* what to do.

I held my model Spitfire tight in my hand as Finn looked at me without speaking.

I stopped breathing.

But then Finn smiled and put his fist to my fist (that is the 3rd time that Finn has done this – we must be very good friends) and started to put the chocolates in order.

I breathed again. It was a very happy day.

Mrs Patel said, 'Shh, don't tell Mr Patel,' and gave us each a Snickers bar and a bag of crisps.

Mr Patel said, 'Shh, don't tell Mrs Patel,' and gave us each a giant bag of Maltesers.

These were 2 good secrets to keep. We smiled.

'Sasha, Finn, Willem – quick come and have a look,' said Mrs Patel, and she pushed my wheelchair to the door. There in the distance was a row of tiny flames. We watched them get nearer and nearer.

Archie was doing a hop and a skip at the front. He was leading a line of people from Tarkey House. They were carrying candles and food. The food was put on the tables and the candles dotted around the estate. It looked very beautiful.

Sasha wheeled me out of the shop. Everyone from both estates formed a circle holding hands. This is called a vigil. Sasha had my right hand and Finn held my left hand, so I did not have to hold a stranger's hand. We all closed our eyes for two minutes exactly. No one spoke, so that we could think our thoughts and pray for the troubles to end.

13

Sasha

The last second of the last minute of our two-minute silence ticked, and everyone dropped hands and we all just stood there smiling at each other. It was proper peaceful. This was a miracle 'cause no one ever shuts their mouths on the Beckham Estate.

Then the peace got smashed, 'cause some random woman from Tarkey House saw Dad and shouted, 'Give us a song then, Fox,' and everyone started chanting, 'Fox, Fox, Fox, Fox.'

Dad rippled back through the years into rock star mode, and punched his fist into the air. Everyone cheered loudly. I ran into Archie's to get his guitar, while someone brought out amps and a mic from who knows where, and Finn helped Archie push his piano out of his front door.

'There you are, Dad,' I said, putting the guitar strap over his neck. 'Show 'em what you can do.'

He winked at me as he grabbed the mic. 'Hello, Beckham Estate and Tarkey House.' The whole place erupted. He struck the first chord on his guitar and the estate exploded into a party.

Dad started singing 'You Got Me Bad' and he looked truly happy for the first time in years. Archie rocked on the piano.

I stretched my hands in the air like everyone else and we were swaying like we was all one.

I looked round me. It looked proper magic with the candles. Our estate was spick and span. Some of the car shells had been moved and people had draped tablecloths over those that were left. I checked in with Willem, to see if all this was doing his head in, but he had his hands in the air too – trying to sing along, but getting the words all wrong. He must be the only person on Planet Earth who don't know them.

Some of the women still had their turban scarves on and it really did look proper nineteen-forties. That's when I thought up my plan.

'Back in a sec,' I said to Willem, and I squeezed behind the piano and ran back into Archie's flat. I came running out a minute later, wearing Rachel's dress and carrying one of the flying hats.

I pulled the flying hat over Willem's head and parked him at the front of the crowd. When Dad saw me, he said, 'Go on,' and held out the mic.

My legs were shaking 'cause of all them people looking at me. Malisha and Tamsin were right at the front of the crowd, having a good old snigger. My face was proper burning up, but I knew what I had to do.

I grabbed the mic, closed my eyes and started the first note of 'Maisy's Rain'. It was my dad's special song; he wrote it for my mum, before she ran off with Ferret the drummer.

When I was a tiny girl, I used to hear my dad crying at night; I used to sneak into his bedroom and snuggle next to him on the pillow and sing it to him till he slept.

It became our song. Then it became the nation's song. Even though Zebra Blue was no more, that song carried on. I suppose, like the Beckham Estate, it just carried on through all its troubles.

Everyone went proper quiet as I began to sing. I opened my eyes and it was like my voice was flying into them, making their troubles fade, just for a minute. Even Malisha and Tamsin had shut their big gobs. I found Finn in the crowd and sang the last line, *'You're under my skin,'* to him. He looked proper gobsmacked, 'cause he hadn't heard me sing before, not really, 'cause I was always scared of making a show of myself.

As the last note flew, the biggest cheer ever smacked the air. I gave Dad back the mic and he played the crowd more Zebra Blue hits: 'Lizzy Sapphire', 'Angel Missy' and 'Go Go Go'.

People were going proper mental.

As Dad took his last bow, a tear trickling down his cheek, the sparkles of his old self vanished into the dark sky. I didn't want the party to end, NOT EVER. I wanted to dance all night, so I ran over to Archie on the piano.

'Play some dance music, Archie,' I whispered, and he struck up his big band sound. I grabbed Gracie and we worked some jitterbug moves like we had done in Archie's flat. Then I did the wheelchair jive with Willem and everyone caught on. Women were falling over each other, running into the flats and coming back with pencil skirts and trilby hats and high-heels and those old-fashioned pinnies and anything that looked vaguely nineteen-forty-ish. They was lending each other red lipstick and giggling, drawing seams up the back of each other's legs. The old lady Archie had helped down the stairs in the fire was dancing with her ginger cat; it was proper funny. Mr Richardson was dancing with Mrs Hubert – ugh gross! My headteacher has no rhythm.

The press were still lurking with cameras, sticking their lenses in people's faces.

Trish had a pink turban to go with her pink trainers. I watched her trying to get Craig, Finn's dad, to dance with her but he shook her off and stomped off, probably to the pub.

I smiled as Gracie grabbed Trish and started to dance with her. Soon Trish was well into it.

She wasn't the only one. People were jiving away their sadness. Their sons and daughters had been dragged off – not to war, like in the nineteen-forties – but down the police station for robbing trainers.

Someone grabbed my hand and whirled me round. It was TJ's cousin, Jaeden. Before I knew it I was jiving faster and faster. My legs were flying, whirling away my strife, stamping and swaying to the rhythm, on and on and on.

The rhythm got faster and faster and louder and

louder, and as I whirled round I looked over at the piano. Archie had gone! There was a bald man playing Archie's piano instead.

I had a proper funny feeling in my gut. Supposing magic man Archie had vanished *puff!* into the thin air. I told myself not to be stupid, but where was he? Without him everything would go back to how it was before. RUBBISH!

'I gotta go, Jaeden,' I said.

He grabbed my hand, but I shook it off.

'Sorry,' I said, and pushed and shoved my way through the jiving crowds searching for Archie – but not finding him anywhere. The graffiti-sprayed walls looked proper eerie in the candlelight.

I reached Dad. His eyes were shut, lost in the music as he played a guitar solo.

'Where did Archie go?' I shouted in his ear.

'Don't know, Sash. He just vanished.'

My gut flipped over. More people joined Dad with guitars and someone was lugging a drum kit.

As the rhythms rocked through me, I pushed past people to get to the flats. I banged on the door of Number One. 'Archie,' I screamed, 'ARCHIE!' But no one answered.

I ran down to the fence protecting his garage project under the flats. I put my hands on the cold metal bars. My eyes pierced the dark, panicking, searching for magic man Archie. But there was nothing but cars.

I heaved myself back through the crowds.

Hip-hop, grunge, R&B and old-time soul hits vibrated through the estate.

'Have you seen Archie?' I asked again and again.

But no one could hear me.

I looked and looked and looked till I could look no more. I got knocked and whirled about, then Finn grabbed my arm.

'Have you seen Archie?' I shouted.

Finn shook his head.

The beats shot through me and I couldn't help it but I started some moves, and we danced and danced and danced with Buster jumping up at us till it got light; and with the music came this drone that got louder and louder and louder. Finn flung me over his shoulder and spun me around. That's when I saw it up in the sky, dancing in the clouds: a Spitfire!

As its propeller spun, the little plane dipped and swooped over the wasteland, lower and lower, a beautiful eagle of the sky. My heart sang as the drone of the engine shook through my bones.

The music petered out and everyone stood still, their gobs open, staring as the Spitfire danced overhead. All you could hear was the drone of the plane and Staffies barking. Buster was going mental so Finn grabbed his collar. I saw Willem flapping his arms and smiling up at the sky. Gracie was stroking the top of his head, tears splashing down her face. The Spitfire swooped lower. It looked as if it was going to land. I ran over to Willem, Gracie and Finn, and grabbed the handles of Willem's wheelchair. We ran right to the edge of the wasteland, feet stampeding behind us as everyone followed. There was a loud gasp as the Spitfire dived through the sky and landed in front of the old youth club. Then, as one, we all crept forwards slowly, slowly till we were surrounding the plane.

It weren't just Gracie crying, a lot of old people were crying. That Spitfire was so beautiful and must have made their war memories come crashing back. I held out my hand to Gracie and she squeezed it hard. She looked at me and whispered, 'The Spitfire, it gave us hope – and we need that right now. Oh Sasha, we need some hope.'

Archie climbed out of the cockpit and stood on the wing.

'Meet Maisy,' he said.

14

WILLEM

Maisy the Spitfire was magnificent. There was silence. No one said any words. I could hear a blackbird sing from the top of the tower block. Gran had her hand on my head, stroking me like I was Buster the dog. She had tears pouring down her face.

I shook her hand off. 'Gran, why are you crying?' I asked. 'Why has the Spitfire made you sad?'

Nosy people turned to look at me.

'Oh, Willem, the Spitfire – it has churned up memories of happiness and sadness, of hard times and the very best times from the past, and mixed them all up and thrown them into today. I'm not sad, I'm moved. Do you understand?'

'Yes,' I said, but it was not a truth.

Then Fox started to clap and everyone joined in and the clapping got louder and louder and people were cheering Maisy the Spitfire.

Sasha wheeled me forwards to look at Maisy. Everyone else kept what my gran calls *a respectful distance.*

Maisy the Spitfire was a 2-seater aeroplane. This means she has 2 cockpits one behind the other. She was a dark grey and green so that in World War 2 she could fly across the English Channel without being detected. She had 14 bullet holes in her side and she was scratched and battered.

'Your Spitfire is very messy, Archie,' I said, 'but I like her a lot.'

'Thank you,' he said, 'Maisy is rather special.'

Archie reached into the cockpit and brought out a newspaper, then jumped down from the wing. He opened up the paper and put it on to my knees.

Sasha leaned over my shoulder and we read the article Archie pointed to.

Millionnaire Dies Leaving Spitfire

Malcolm Inglesfield, the eccentric millionnaire, died peacefully in his sleep, leaving a Spitfire known as Maisy among his possessions. He had just had the Spitfire converted into a two-seater, but had not yet started on the rest of the extensive renovations that the aeroplane needed when he sadly passed away.

He left a provision in his will that the Spitfire should pass on to someone whom his solicitor deemed to have a connection with the aeroplane. The Spitfire, known as Maisy, has passed on to Archie Dobbs, whose mother Rachel Dobbs was part of the ATA and ferried Spitfires during World War Two.

Archie Dobbs said, 'This is a dream come true. I shall work hard to return Maisy to her former glory in honour of my mother, Rachel.'

'I thought, my dears, you would like to help me with the final touches, and help make Maisy into the fine old girl she was.'

Sasha did not say any words. She walked over to the Spitfire and reached out and touched the wing and smiled the smile of an angel.

'Yes please, Archie. I would like that very much,' I said.

Suddenly men with cameras were all around us, pushing and shoving. One man with sticking-out black hair banged into my wheelchair so hard it tilted sideways.

'Oi, watch yourself,' shouted Sasha. My fingers started to jiggle, my brain tangled and my world started to melt.

I could hear Sasha shouting.

I stretched my hand out through the fuzzy greyness to find my dog-friend. My hand was licked, then Buster was climbing on my knees and the greyness vanished. My brain untangled and my hands were still.

I could hear Finn shouting, 'Buster, come back here.' But Buster ignored him and stayed with me.

I saw Archie talking to the men with cameras. I put my hand on my head; I still had Archie's flying helmet on.

And then Archie handed us gloves and a flying helmet for Sasha.

Archie and the man lifted me out of my wheelchair, and carried me on to Maisy's wing. They pulled the canopy back and helped me hop down into the cockpit of the magnificent Spitfire.

I breathed Maisy in. She smelled of oil and old leather. I liked her perfume. Sasha climbed into the cockpit after me. We both squashed up on the front bucket seat. Sasha was on my lap. Archie had packed his parachute inside the bucket seat. This is what pilots in World War 2 sat on. It is not as comfortable as my gran's sofa. Then Buster scrambled up into the back seat and the camera people laughed and took lots of photographs. I took my flying helmet off and put it on Buster so he would be correctly dressed.

The cameras kept on clicking, taking pictures of me and my 2 friends (1 amber and 1 green). I was happy so it was easy to smile. I do not think Mrs Hubert, my teacher, would count being friends with a Spitfire for my homework because an aeroplane is an inanimate object, even though this one has a girl's name, Maisy.

When the clicking stopped, the camera people packed up their cameras and went away. Sasha and

I smiled at each other. I rested my head against the leather head buffer. It rustled. I do not like rustling. I put my hand behind my head and felt a small rip in the side of the headrest. With my finger, I felt inside and touched what was making the rustling noise. I pulled it out. It was a bit of faded yellow paper.

'It is rubbish,' I said. Buster went to grab it in his mouth.

'STOP,' yelled Sasha. She snatched the paper and smoothed it out on her knee.

I peeped over her shoulder.

It was a note. It said:

Rachel, my angel of the sky,
will you marry me?

A note from Sasha

Cold tiptoed up my spine.

The note in Rachel's handbag wasn't the last note – this was. Robert wanted to marry her!

'Archie,' I shouted, scrambling out of the cockpit and climbing on to the wing. 'Archie, please come here quick.'

'What is it, my dear?' said Archie, running over.

'Look,' said Sasha. 'Look – it's Robert's handwriting. It's a note to Rachel. It was inside this tear in the headrest. This was one of his secret places. He must have flown this very Spitfire. Rachel never got it because he never came back. Oh Archie, she never ever knew he wanted to marry her.' It proper broke my heart.

'We will never know the whole truth,' said Archie.

'Don't look sad, Sasha,' said Willem. 'If Rachel had married Robert, then she would not have married Stanley, and Archie, our friend, would not have been born.'

Sometimes Willem has pure wisdom.

'Those twenty-one days they were sweethearts . . .

my mother always said they were the happiest days of her life,' said Archie.

'Please put it in Rachel's handbag in the wooden chest, with the other note from Robert,' I said, handing it to Archie. 'Keep Robert's note safe.'

Shivers jitterbugged through me. Aunty Lou and Gran had appeared behind Archie. Aunty Lou helped me down from the Spitfire and put one of her cardigans round my shivering shoulders.

'I think all this excitement has been a bit too much for you,' she said, giving me a hug.

'Gran,' said Willem,' I love this Spitfire, Maisy. She is old, like you.'

Aunty Lou and I looked at each other and choked back our laughs.

'Why are you laughing? I was not making a joke,' said Willem, as all the people from the Beckham and Tarkey House estates crowded round, taking photographs of Maisy on their phones.

'How about it, then?' said Archie. 'Would you like to help me restore Maisy to her former glory?'

I winked at Willem. 'You bet,' I said. 'Just try to stop us. Maisy's going to look proper sparkling by the time we've finished.'

And suddenly Finn was there. His eyes were shining. He said, 'I wanna help with Maisy. Get her looking slick. You gotta let me help.'

Archie's eyes twinkled. Willem smiled. I shivered. I don't know why, but uneasiness knocked at the door of my heart as I looked into Finn's eyes.

15

Sasha

I woke up in my own bed. My head was banging. Then the words 'LAST CHANCE' and 'MONDAY' smacked my brain. Today was the day I was summoned to MR RICHARDSON'S OFFICE. My gut fell a million miles.

I could hear Dad clattering around in the kitchen, singing 'Maisy's Rain'. I could still smell the minging smoke-smell from the fire.

I stretched out to look at the time on my phone, then remembered it needed charging, so I rolled out of bed and grabbed my dressing gown from the floor and went into the kitchen.

'Do you want some toast, Sash?' said Dad, from behind his *Gig Weekly* music magazine.

I robbed an already-buttered piece off his plate and looked at the clock. IT WAS NINE O'CLOCK.

I was meant to be at school this minute, sitting in registration, not at home eating toast.

'DAD, WHY DIDN'T YOU WAKE ME?' I yelled.

My head banged harder.

'I thought you could do with a bit of a sleep,' he said, still reading.

I grabbed *Gig Weekly* out of his hands, and threw it on the table. 'DAD, it's school, I have to be there. It's the law or something.'

I stormed out of the room, banging the door.

My head properly throbbed as I ran back to my bedroom, falling headlong over Dad's old guitar that he'd gone and left in the hallway.

It made a clanging sound, which made my head explode more.

'Right, school clothes,' I said out loud, and there they were, still kicked in the corner, where I had left them before I'd gone to the hospital on Friday. I had the quickest sprinkle in the shower, grabbed a towel, and ran back to my bedroom and struggled into a damp shirt off the clothes horse, and my creased school skirt and jumper from the corner. I grabbed my school bag and ran. I felt disgusting. THIS DID NOT PROMISE TO BE A GOOD DAY.

'Laters, Dad,' I shouted, banged the front door and ran along the balcony. As I ran past Finn's flat I could hear his dad, Craig, shouting. I sprinted down to the eighth floor. I pressed the lift button but the stupid thing wouldn't come, so I kicked the stupid, stupid, stupid door and ran all the way down to the courtyard. By the time I got there, I felt proper puffed out.

Gracie was standing in the doorway of Number One. 'Sasha,' she shouted and beckoned me over.

'I'm late, Gracie,' I shouted.

'I know,' she shouted back. 'Willem won't go to school without you. He's got himself into one of his states.'

I ran over to Number One. Willem was sitting in the armchair; he had an old wooden crutch like the ones soldiers had in war films. It must have been Archie's. His finger was doing that shaky thing. I felt proper guilty.

'Sasha, today is my Science test and I am going to be late. You are not in the top set for Science, so you do not have a test, but I do and it is very important. I waited for you. We are meant to be at school at nine. It is now nine forty-five.'

My headache explosion reached the sky. I was

going to be even later now. The words 'LAST CHANCE, LAST CHANCE, LAST CHANCE' kicked my brain.

'Willem, can we use your wheelchair? It will be quicker if I push you.'

'No,' said Willem. 'Today I will use the crutch.'

'Where's Archie?' I asked. 'Do any of his cars work enough to give us a lift?'

'He's been called out on business,' said Gracie.

'Your clothes are all creased, Sasha,' said Willem.

'Thanks,' I said.

'It's quite all right,' said Willem. I forgot Willem don't do sarcasm. This day was getting more and more messed up.

'Willem, I'm taking the wheelchair with us, whether you like it or not,' I told him.

I dumped our school bags in the chair and pushed it beside Willem, who was hobbling oh so slowly, slowly. I WAS GOING TO BE IN SUCH TROUBLE. When we were halfway across the courtyard, Malisha tottered past us all dressed up in jeans, a black top and high-heels.

They wear their own clothes down the pupil referral unit and don't start till ten. There really is no justice on this planet.

'You going to school like that?' she sniggered. 'Tramp,' she said under her breath, but loud enough for me to hear her.

'My clothes may be creased, but at least I've got a school to go to, eh?'

Malisha stormed off.

'Maybe your mum could give me one of your old school uniforms,' I shouted after her. 'She should open a stall down Camden Market, selling off all your old school uniforms from the schools you've been chucked out of.'

Then I felt sick 'cause today might be the day when I get chucked out too and end up at the pupil referral unit with her.

'Come on, Willem, can't you limp faster?'

'No,' said Willem. 'You should have come for me at eight-thirty.'

I was just thinking this day couldn't get any worse when from behind me I heard, 'Wait up, Sash.' I turned round and Finn was running towards us.

'Oh terrific!' I groaned, but MY BRAIN STARTED TO TICK. If I arrived late with Finn then Mrs Hubert would assume things, but if I was with Willem I could say I was helping Willem to school, being community-minded, like she is always telling us to be RIGHT, SORTED, that's how I would play it.

I smiled at Finn. 'You better run ahead, it's going to take us ages. I don't want to get you into trouble. Why aren't you at school already?'

'Cause I had issues to deal with. You know how it is. I've texted you about a million times, Sash. I need to copy your homework.'

'What homework?' OH NO, THAT'S ANOTHER THING I'D BE IN TROUBLE FOR. I'D FORGOTTEN.

'I will help you,' said Willem.

'Nice one,' said Finn.

And would you believe it? Finn and Willem started having this whole conversation about engines as we crossed the wasteland. I shoved the wheelchair handles into Finn's hands and stomped ahead over the bumpy ground. I couldn't see Maisy anywhere! What had Archie done with her?

Then something caught my eye through the window of the old youth club. I ran over and jumped, grabbing the window ledge and scuffing my knee on the wall as I heaved myself up till I was sitting on it. I used the sleeve of my jumper to wipe a hole in the mucky window to get a look.

All the partitions that had made up the different rooms had gone.

Some planks of wood were still leaning up against the corner. There was an old sign, *Coke 60p, Crisps 50p*, dangling down from one drawing pin. There was no pool table or vending machines any more, but instead there was Maisy, looking beautiful in her new home. It was proper perfect. The wall at the end had huge garage doors which they used to keep open in the summer for barbecues and things. Now they were shut to keep Maisy safe.

I jumped down off the windowsill and caught up with the boys, who were still talking about engines.

Then Finn spots a bunch of Beckham Street Boyz hangers-on and just lets go of the wheelchair and walks off, mid-sentence, like he ain't even with us. Like me and Willem don't exist.

Willem's face crumpled, 'cause he don't understand the complexities of the mixed-upness that is Finn.

As we turned the corner it seemed like the whole school was outside on the pavement. There was a notice on the gate:

School closed for emergency measures.

YES! Happiness zinged up through my toes to my head, which had stopped banging. Result! Result! Result!

'But what about my Science test?' said Willem, taking his model Spitfire out of his pocket and spinning the propeller fast.

Only Willem could be sad about not taking a Science test!

Policemen were crawling everywhere. Mr Richardson was talking to a bunch of teachers at the school gate. Then he looked proper stressed as he watched loads of people in suits walk through the school gates. The mayor got out of a shiny black Bentley. And then I saw Archie.

I ran up to him. 'What's going on, Archie?'

'Hello, my dear. They're having a meeting about the riots,' he said. 'It looks like they are going to go on for a few days. I am so sorry. If I'd only been told sooner they were holding them here, I could have stopped you and Willem coming all this way. I phoned Gracie, but you'd already left.'

'It's all right, Archie,' I said, and gave him a smacker kiss on the cheek and a hug. He looked proper shocked. I laughed and started doing this mad dance of happiness, like mad Mrs Cummings, who used to live at Number Twelve, before the men in white coats carted her off.

'Don't count your chickens before they've hatched,' said Archie. 'Look.' He pointed behind me.

Mrs Hubert was clapping her hands and shouting, 'MY CLASS, OVER HERE, PLEASE. COLLECT YOUR HOMEWORK ASSIGNMENT.'

I groaned, and walked back to Willem and helped him hop over to stand with the rest of our class – well, the ones who hadn't been arrested, anyway. We stood in front of Mrs Hubert, who started handing out sheets of paper.

'Right, class, you are not to waste your time at home. I want you to work in small groups on a project. The theme is: How Numeracy Helps People in Real Life. Each group must choose a topic to illustrate this and present it to the class. You'll find all the information you need on these handouts so DON'T LOSE THEM! You have six whole weeks to work on your presentation, SO THEY HAD BETTER BE GOOD. You can decide who you are going to work with and start researching now, while the school is

closed. Oh and Sasha Barton, YOU NEEDN'T THINK
THAT I'VE FORGOTTEN THAT YOU RAN OUT OF MY
CLASS. YOUR BEHAVIOUR THIS TERM HAS BEEN
DIGUSTING.'

She was shouting so loud everyone stopped talking
and turned to stare. I felt proper shamed.

'Please, Miss, I—'

'Be quiet, Sasha. Mr Richardson is far too busy to
deal with you today. You need to think long and hard
about your future at this—'

'Please, Miss, PLEASE,' I begged. 'I will work really
hard at this numbers project thing. PLEASE.'

There was this deathly quiet like the whole street
had their eyeballs on me, waiting for Mrs Hubert's
next move.

Then through the silence cut Willem's voice. 'I will
work with Sasha,' he said. 'We will do a good
presentation. She is my new friend.'

I felt a proper warm glow. If I worked with Willem,
I knew I could, for once in my life, do a piece of work
I'd be proud of, and get a million merit marks.

Mrs Hubert sighed and looked from me to Willem
then back to me again.

'Very well. This project is extra important for

you. You must use it to REDEEM YOURSELF. Do you understand, Sasha?'

'Yes, Miss . . .'

Everyone stopped being nosy and went about their business.

'We can do the Spitfire,' said Willem. 'The pilots had to be able to understand the numbers on the dials in the cockpit.'

'Willem, you're a genius,' I said, having a quick look at the handout. 'It says we can use photographs and bring evidence in to illustrate the presentation. You can talk about how they were built, and I will talk about Rachel and the Spitfire women pilots and—'

'And I'll talk about restoring the Spitfire,' said Finn, walking up behind me.

I ignored him.

'It will be excellent, Willem, you and me together,' I said.

'I could do a painting to show what the Spitfire markings were like,' said Finn.

I ignored him again.

'And I am going to talk about mechanics of flight; Willem's just told me all about it,' went on Finn.

'You!' I spun round to face him. 'WHAT'S IT GOT TO

DO WITH YOU, FINN? You didn't want to know us a minute ago. I'm working with Willem. Not you.'

'Sash, I've got to work with you. TJ and Laurence are locked up, innit. I got no one else to work with.'

'Oh, we are so honoured, I am sure,' I said, doing my best sarky voice that even Mrs Hubert couldn't beat.

'Yes, we would be very honoured if you would join our group,' said Willem. 'We can be the Spitfire Club.'

And with that, all my happiness vanished from the day and my dreams of getting a million merit marks flew up into the clouds.

'I am going to teach the class how to fly. I will use examples of early flying machines,' said Willem.

A nasty smile flickered on Finn's lips. He didn't think I saw it. But I did.

16

WILLEM

Mrs Hubert would not let me past her to get into school to complete my Science test.

She said, 'The school is closed for everyone – and that includes you, Willem Smith.'

'But, Mrs Hubert, I have done my homework and made 2 friends.'

She walked away from me. She does not have good listening skills.

There was nothing for it; I would have to head back to the Beckham Estate. My foot was throbbing. I moved the bags and sat in the wheelchair and balanced the crutch across my knees.

Sasha smiled. 'Bet you're glad I brought the chair now, aren't you?'

'Thank you, Sasha,' I said. 'You were right.'

My gran said that is called being *gracious*.

Sasha pushed me and Finn walked beside us. We past a burned-out Morris Minor. Some of the shops by the school had boards on the front windows and people with sad faces were sweeping up outside.

Now that Finn had stopped making me jump off things and wanted to work in my group for the presentation I could do 2 homeworks at once.

1 Do an excellent presentation on the Spitfire and get a lot of merit marks.
2 Show Mrs Hubert that I am friends with Finn. (I will point out to Mrs Hubert that making friends with Finn should give me a lot of merit marks, as he used to hate me. I would like to win the Headteacher's Cup for Excellence for the 2nd year running, for getting the most merit marks in the whole school.)

Sasha tipped my wheelchair on its back wheels, and whirled me round in a U-shape to block Finn's path.

'We ain't going further, Finn, till you promise on your life that you will not mess up our Spitfire presentation. Do you hear me? 'Cause even though I got love for you in my heart, I got uneasiness about your school skills.'

'Finn,' I said, trying to help my friend Sasha explain, 'you are not very clever in your lessons. You do not get good marks in class. We want you to try really hard. Then we can get lots of merit marks and Sasha will not be in trouble with Mrs Hubert for running out of school.'

Finn's face flickered into expressions I could not understand. For 1 second I thought he was angry, but then he smiled and had a happy face on.

'Look, I'll work hard. To get you out of trouble, Sash. I promise on my life.'

'You better keep your word, Finn. I mean it – no jokes,' said Sasha, turning my chair back round the right way and running with it. Finn ran and grabbed the chair off her and pushed me faster.

They took turns pushing faster and faster until it was like flying, with the wind pulling my cheeks back, and we were laughing, my 2 friends and me. Then I heard barking, and Buster was running towards me and jumped on my lap, and we stopped to give my dog-friend kisses and cuddles.

'Buster!' said Finn, 'How did you get out? I shut you in the kitchen. I swear I did.' He phoned Trish to tell her that Buster was safe with us, his friends, because it is responsible pet ownership to always know where your dog is.

Then Finn pushed me extra-fast with Buster barking as he rode in the wheelchair, flying with me.

When we reached the Beckham Estate, there were police everywhere and vanloads of kids from our estate were being unloaded and marched into Archie's garage project under our flats.

I put my hand into my pocket and held on to my model Spitfire tight.

A police car drove up and dropped Archie off. I shouted, 'Archie, we are over here,' but he did not hear me.

'Come on,' said Sasha. 'Let's go and have a nosy.'

Archie was standing on a wooden platform, near the back of the garage. There were 7 old cars in the spaces amongst the pillars that held the flats up above our heads. 1 Aston Martin, 2 Fords, 3 Volvos and 1 Mini. The cars were battered and untidy. There was a bench of tools behind Archie. A policeman with ginger hair was handing him a bundle of papers. They must have been documents with the names of the boys and girls who had been arrested.

He turned and glared at both gangs. 'Behave,' he said, 'or you'll be back in court in the blink of an eye.' I think that policeman was exaggerating. It is a 20-minute drive to the courts on Bakewell Road. Then all the policemen left.

The T Crew were standing on the left side of the garage, facing the Beckham Street Boyz, who were all on the right. They had hate faces on. Nobody spoke. The silence crackled.

Finn walked over to stand at the front of his gang, the Beckham Street Boyz. Buster jumped off my knees and followed his master. TJ and Laurence pushed their way to the front of the crowd to stand on either side of Finn.

The 2 gangs glared at each other. I spun the propeller on my Spitfire. Still nobody spoke.

Archie coughed and broke the silence. 'Righty-ho,' he said, and waved the papers the policeman gave him in the air.

'Righty-ho, righty-ho, righty-ho,' mocked Richie Lane. The T Crew sniggered.

Finn squared up to Richie. 'Don't you disrespect, Archie,' he said. All the Beckham Street Boyz started moving in behind Finn. Then there were kids moving everywhere, getting too close to me, and I couldn't tell who was in what gang, and there was whispering and shouting and bad noise all around me. My brain was tangled. They were getting closer and closer. There was going to be a battle. Buster whined and hid behind Finn's legs. My world melted as I shut my eyes.

Then a voice in my ear said, 'Willem, WILLEM! It's OK, I've got you.'

It was Sasha and my wheelchair was dragged backwards. I opened my eyes. The T Crew and Beckham Street Boyz were facing each other, ready to fight. This had to stop. IT HAD TO STOP! I shoved my model Spitfire back in my pocket.

'This is our territory,' said Finn.

'Finn, no,' shouted Sasha.

'SASHA, PUSH ME THROUGH THE MIDDLE.

NOW!' I said.

Sasha did, ploughing through the 2 gangs, and I forced my jiggling fingers out to the side till my arm wings were stretched and droned like a Spitfire. Sasha joined in. It worked. Richie Lane and Finn stumbled back out of the path of my wheelchair Spitfire.

Sasha helped me out of my wheelchair and handed me the crutch. I hopped on to the wooden platform and stood on one side of Archie. Sasha stood on the other.

'This garage is mutual territory,' said Archie. 'I will not tolerate gang warfare on this project. Do you all understand me?'

Nobody spoke. The silence crackled louder. My Spitfire arms shook.

'You have a choice,' said Archie. 'Let me teach you about the running of an engine. I will show you all how to strip down an engine and build it up again, then you will have a trade to be proud of. You will learn to build cars, not destroy them. That is choice 1. Choice 2 is that I send you back to jail. What's it to be?'

Still, nobody spoke. All you could hear was

munch, crunch, munch, munch as Richie Lane ate a packet of pickled onion Monster Munch with his mouth open. He does not have manners. The smell made my nose itch.

Crunch, munch, munch crunch.

The word 'silence' crackled louder and louder and louder. Then Buster ran over to the T Crew and stood in front of Richie Lane and begged for a pickled onion Monster Munch.

'Buster, come back here,' Finn shouted, bright red in the face.

Buster ignored Finn. My gran would have said *you could hear a pin drop*. I heard Sasha gasp. I think Buster was feeling very brave as there were no other Staffordshire bull terriers in the garage. He does not know that the T Crew and the Beckham Street Boyz hate each other. Buster just wanted to eat some Monster Munch.

'Buster!' Finn yelled.

Buster started doing a dog dance on his hind legs and howling.

Sasha started laughing. That made me start laughing. Then Richie Lane started laughing and gave Buster some Monster Munch. Then Finn started laughing, and soon everyone was laughing. Buster danced and rolled over and did tricks for more Monster Munch. I think he should go on *Britain's Got Talent.*

Archie did a jump and little jig in the air. His eyes twinkled. 'I guess it's choice 1 then,' he said. 'Learn to build an engine.'

Archie started handing out overalls and put people in groups, mixing the T Crew with the Beckham Street Boyz. Sasha ran over and whispered in Archie's ear, then ran back to me. She had keys in her hand.

'I've told him about our Spitfire presentation,' said Sasha. 'Come on.'

As she wheeled me out of the garage and bumped me over the wasteland, Finn joined us. He was carting buckets with sponges and overalls.

'Where are we going to?' I asked.

'You'll see,' said Sasha.

I do not like surprises.

We stopped outside the old youth club. Sasha put the key in the garage door and turned it. Finn heaved the doors up. I put my hands over my ears to shut out the rattling.

There was Maisy the Spitfire. She had her very own hangar in this deserted building.

Finn whistled. I smiled. This was a good surprise.

Sasha spun around laughing, with her arms outstretched. Then she held hands with Finn and me so we were in a circle.

'We are the top secret Spitfire Club,' she whispered. 'Apart from Archie, only we 3 may enter here. We are to keep this a proper secret. Agreed?'

'Agreed,' Finn and I whispered back.

There was a barking outside and Buster hurtled in and crashed into my legs.

'And Buster,' I said. 'He can be a member too.' Finn laughed, but I had not made a joke.

Sasha grabbed hold of his front paws. 'Buster, you are now a member of the Spitfire Club.' He gave her a dog-lick kiss on the nose.

Finn went to a tap in the corner and filled the buckets with water.

'Right, you 2, snap to it. We've got work to do. We've got 6 weeks. We gotta clean Maisy, give the old girl a bath,' he said, patting the Spitfire like she was Buster.

Sasha stopped laughing. 'It's gotta be good, our

presentation. It's gotta be the best out of everyone's. I am on my last chance. '

'Finn,' I said holding out my hand, 'I need your phone to take photographs of Maisy while she is dirty.'

'Before and after photographs! Good thinking, Willem,' said Sasha.

Finn hesitated, then grinned and gave me his Samson S4 Galaxy.

I took 6 photographs.

Finn handed out overalls to stop our clothes getting dirty. I do not like wearing clothes that are not mine, but I wanted to give Maisy a bath and make her beautiful so I swallowed and put them on. Sasha helped me. Sasha scrambled on to the wing and climbed down into the cockpit to clean inside. Finn climbed after her and started washing Maisy's wing. I hopped along with my crutch, sponging her body down. Maisy started to shine.

I had done my homework for Mrs Hubert. I had made 2 friends of my own age. I was a member of a top secret club. I had never belonged to anything in my 12 years 4 months and 3 days of being on this planet – apart from the library. If this was what having friends was like, I liked it. I felt happy.

THE TOP SECRET RULES OF THE SPITFIRE CLUB

1. Only members of the Spitfire Club are
permitted in our headquarters (Maisy's hangar).

2. Members of the Spitfire Club shall not be
permitted into the headquarters without knocking
3 times and saying the password Maisy's Rain.

3. The code word for a very urgent private
conversation is 'scramble'*.

4. 'Chocks Away'** will be said at the end of
every Spitfire Club meeting.

5. No members of the Spitfire Club shall divulge
its secrets.

Signed

Willem Edward Smith

Sasha Barton

Finn Mason

WILLEM'S NOTES:
*SCRAMBLE was a code word used in World War 2.
It was a signal for the pilots to run to their
Spitfires and take off into the sky as soon as
possible. This means it is a very good word
for urgency.
**Chocks are the wooden blocks that are placed in
front of the wheels of the Spitfire. They are
moved before take-off. It is a good word to say
as a signal that we are taking off by foot before
we meet again.

17

Sasha

Week 1

And that was us, the Spitfire Club: Finn, Willem, me –
and Buster, of course.

School opened today after the emergency
measures riot meetings, worst luck!

Since I was on my last chance, I was sitting in
Maths next to Willem at the front, instead of at the
back with Finn. Hopefully that way I would not get into
trouble and would learn something about Maths.

I couldn't wait to get to the Spitfire Club that
evening!

Mrs Hubert was writing more sums that I couldn't
understand on the white board when a ball of paper
hit me on the back of the head. I turned round and saw

Finn pointing to the empty seat next to him.

'SIT HERE,' he mouthed. He did not look happy. I shrugged my shoulders and turned back round to do my work.

Fractions

Sasha's Spitfire Club House List

1. Sweep floor.
2. Ask Gracie, Trish and Archie if they have any old cushions.
3. Take some from sofa at home. (Dad will not notice.)
4. Take mugs and plates from home and spare kettle.
5. Take as much as I can carry from home. (Dad still won't notice.)
6. Get some

Mrs Hubert would not give me my list back till the end of the Maths lesson, even though I blatantly told her it was to help with my presentation.

'FRACTIONS,' she said, banging her fist on the desk.

It's a good thing I've got a good memory as to what was on that list 'cause I carried on planning in my head. Some things in life are more important than fractions!

As soon as school was over, I grabbed the key off Archie and dragged Dad's old suitcase full of everything I could rob from our flat across the wasteland to our top secret Spitfire Club House.

I was the first to arrive. Finn was in detention and Willem had stayed behind at school to ask for extra Physics homework. I started to get to work, making our Club House look comfy.

An hour later, I was lying on my belly on Maisy's wing eating a cheese and pickle sandwich, admiring our top secret Spitfire Club House. If I do say so myself, I've made it look proper smart.

I've swept the floor and stacked a load of beer crates I found in the corner and covered them with this purple crushed velvet material that I found in the flat. It must have been left by my mum.

It's weird, but there seemed to be fewer planks of wood in the corner than before.

I set up the kettle and mugs and plates and, if I'm honest, half our kitchen contents on a table in the corner. It looked proper cosy.

Bang! I jumped as a football crashed against the door, followed by voices.

'Finn – yeah, we need to find him.'

And then another voice that sounded like Laurence. 'Things kicking off with T Crew again.'

Bang! Bang! Bang! They kicked the ball against the door, over and over again.

I didn't like it. I didn't want them to look through the window and find me here. I pulled the canopy back and something made me look up. A young girl I recognized from our estate, with raven-black hair and a proper cheeky grin, was peeping through the window. Our eyes met.

'Nell,' called a boy's voice. There was a scrabbling sound and she disappeared.

I quickly climbed into Maisy's cockpit and curled into a ball.

I know this may sound proper daft, but I felt like Rachel was in that cockpit with me, putting her arms round me, keeping me safe.

Bang, bang, bang, went the ball against the door, harder and harder. Then, 'I'm starving – going to Bernie's to get a number two meal. Coming?'

I breathed out as the voices moved away from the

door, with the sound of the football being kicked across the wasteland.

And then immediately there was a triple knock on the door.

'Maisy's Rain,' came a voice from outside.

I climbed out of the cockpit on to the wing and down to the ground.

'Sasha, quick.' It was Finn.

I pushed the shutter door up and in hurtled Buster, followed by Finn, pushing the wheelchair. In it sat what looked like a very round old man, with his mouth covered in an old scarf and hat pulled down over his eyes.

I quickly closed the door.

Finn started laughing as he pulled the old man's hat off and Willem's face smiled up at me.

'It is me, Willem Edward Smith,' he said.

'Beckham Boyz are everywhere, wanting to chat. I told 'em I had to get my old uncle to the doctor's,' said Finn.

Willem struggled out of an old coat and loads of pink and green cushions fell around him as he undid the buttons.

'Gran and Trish have given us these for our Spitfire

Club House,' said Willem.

His hands were doing that shaking thing. I put my hand over them. Wearing that disguise must have been proper stressful for Willem. Finn gave me a funny look.

I grabbed the cushions and arranged them on top of the purple crushed velvet that covered the crates. It looked startling. Our own Spitfire Club House sofa.

'My right foot feels ten per cent better and my left cut big toe feels twelve point five per cent better,' Willem said, hobbling over to help me.

Buster ran round and round Maisy in circles and snatched one of the pink cushions from our sofa and ran off with it in his mouth.

Buster loves to be the centre of attention. He will do anything for cuddles. Finn chased after him, followed by me and Willem hobbling along behind. Soon we were screaming with laughter, trying to get the cushion off him.

'It's me – Archie,' we heard over a knock at the door. I ran to let him in.

'Are you ready to get started working on Maisy?'

Archie showed us how to fill in bullet holes and check cable runs and hydraulics. We painted and polished and tinkered with Maisy. She was like the fifth member of our club. It was brilliant.

Every evening after school that week, we met there in our Club House. My favourite place in the world was to lie on my belly on Maisy's wing, eating my sandwiches and just chatting rubbish about the day with Finn and Willem. When it got dark outside we'd shout, 'Chocks away,' and go back home to bed, shutting Maisy up for the night, till the next day's meeting of the Spitfire Club.

But then on the Friday, Finn arrived looking proper edgy. He had only just started working on Maisy when his phone buzzed.

'Gotta go, Sash, sorry,' he said, walking towards the door. But I stepped in and snatched his stupid phone and threw it in the corner.

'That's out of order, Sasha,' shouted Finn.

'Stay, please,' I said. 'Don't go getting into more trouble. These days have been just the best ever. Stay, I'm begging you. Stay with the Spitfire Club.'

I grabbed his hand, but he snatched it away.

'You got no idea how hard it's been to get here every night,' he shouted. 'The Beckham Boyz are everywhere, Sash, I can't get away from it. I come out of my flat and there's TJ and Laurence waiting for me. The lift door opens and one of the elders want to talk. Beckham Boyz on all the landings in the stairwell, legs out, stopping my steps to reach you. Disguising Willem was a last resort. Working on Maisy is the only time . . . the only time . . .'

'You get brain space,' I finished for him.

Finn nodded, his face crumpled. I held out my arms but he snatched his phone up and ran out of the door and across the wasteland. Buster followed him, barking.

'He forgot to say "Chocks away",' said Willem.

I had almost forgotten Willem was there.

Willem
Week 2

On Saturday morning at 10.16 a.m., Archie and I sat in Maisy's cockpit, and he went through the pre-flight checks with me. These are very important for a Spitfire pilot to know. I learned about throttle friction and propeller pitch control. We checked that all the flight controls were in good working order.

Finn should have been there; he is the 3rd member of the Spitfire Club.

I asked Sasha if she had seen him but she did not answer me. She just shrugged her shoulders and asked Archie lots of questions as she painted Maisy.

'Archie,' she said, 'why were the Spitfires painted dark grey and green?'

'For camouflage,' answered Archie. Then she lay on our sofa drinking tea that I had made her and writing notes for our Spitfire presentation.

As I dipped my spoon alternately between my bowl of Rice Krispies and bowl of milk at breakfast on Sunday morning, I assessed that my foot hurt 72% less and my big toe 47.2% less than the second after it had first snapped when I had jumped off the wall.

I hobbled across the wasteland for our Spitfire Club meeting. I have an appointment with Doctor Sergeant a week on Monday at 2.45 p.m. where I will find out if it is better.

I knocked 3 times. 'Maisy's Rain,' I whispered.

Sasha opened the door.

'Come on in.' She smiled her angel smile and

started taking lots of photographs of me with Maisy while we were waiting for Archie. I was happy.

At 11.23 a.m. Archie arrived. He gave me a present, even though it is not my birthday. He had the old operational notes that the Air Transport Auxiliary were given in World War 2 with information on 'How to Fly the Spitfire'. They were called white notes by the ATA because they are in a white cover.

'No Finn?' I heard Archie ask Sasha as I started to read. She shook her head with her sad face on.

Monday was a happy day – when I knocked 3 times and said our secret password 'Maisy's Rain', Finn opened the door.

Buster ran up and gave me a dog kiss on the hand. It is good to report that our 3rd and 4th members of the Spitfire Club are back. Sasha had what my gran calls *a spring in her step* (this does not mean that she had metal coils attached to her feet, it means that she was happy to see Finn at our Spitfire Club meeting). Finn looked tired but worked hard on our presentation on Maisy and followed my instructions. He is a good friend.

But at school on Tuesday I came out of the library, after I had spent lunch hour studying Spitfire facts, and saw Finn leaning against the wall of the Art block.

'Finn,' I shouted. 'Finn!' But he started walking off. 'Finn, did you know there were 21,351 Spitfires built during the war?' I limped after him.

But Finn just walked faster.

Sasha was walking towards me so I stopped to tell her about my problem.

'Sasha,' I said, 'I need to do my homework. I NEED TO prove to Mrs Hubert that I have made 2 friends my own age. Why does Finn not talk to me at school? We are the Spitfire Club.'

'Oh, Willem,' said Sasha, 'it's proper difficult to explain the mixed-upness that is Finn.'

I thought about this problem for the rest of the week and wrote Mrs Hubert a letter and put it on her desk.

Sasha
Week 3

I saw Willem put a note on Mrs Hubert's messy desk. I was curious, so I sneaked a peek.

18th Floor
Flat 103 Beckham Estate
Beckham Street
Camden Town
London
NW1 7AD

Dear Mrs Hubert,

I am not sure if I have done my making 2 friends of my own age homework. This is the 1st homework ever that I am not sure if I have completed. Please will you give me equations like the rest of the class next time. I know when equations are finished.

The task was to make 2 friends my own age. I keep trying to talk to you about this but you do not have good listening skills. I thought if I wrote you a letter you might read it and take notice.

I have done ½ my homework as Sasha Barton is now my friend. I also am friends with Buster who is a Staffordshire bull terrier and a Spitfire called Maisy. I know that you will not count these. I have made friends with Finn Mason. We are only friends on the Beckham Estate. At school he does not talk to me. Does this count? I know that you like proof that homework is finished. I would be very grateful if you could make time to talk to me about this problem as I would like to complete my homework.

Your pupil,

Willem Edward Smith

Lovely Willem, with his proper good heart. All he wants to do is show Mrs Hubert that he has made two friends his own age. Well, he's definitely made one: me.

At Spitfire Club I made sure that I was a better person and that I was the best friend I could possibly be to my lovely Willem. Every day after our work on Maisy was over for the night, we'd say 'Chocks away' and would play Fetch with Buster over the wasteland before heading up home in the stinking lift.

Every night when we reached floor eleven, Finn would give me that look of his and say, 'Sash, come into ours. We can have chips.' My knees would go funny for one second – then I would think of Buster licking the potatoes to make me keep my resolve.

'No, thanks, Finn,' I'd say. 'I gotta see Willem home.'

As the lift door closed, Finn would kick it. The idiot. It wasn't the least bit funny and the sound of that clanging metal made Willem's hand do that shaky thing, so he'd spin the propeller of his model Spitfire till we reached floor eighteen.

Gracie always had a cup of tea and a hug waiting for me. Archie would often be there. He must like hugs and cups of tea too.

On Friday I saw Willem with a smile on his face, even though I had just seen Finn rushing away down the corridor past the Science labs as Willem tried to tell him yet another Spitfire fact.

'What's up, Willem?' I said. 'Share the joy.'

'I have joy,' said Willem. 'Even though Finn will not talk to me at school, at least I have not had to jump off walls. I have not had to jump off walls for three weeks, two hours and thirty seconds. So that makes him a sort of friend.'

That cut my heart into tiny pieces and scattered it all over the floor.

'Oh, Willem,' I said and gave him a gentle kiss on the cheek, just as Finn walked back round the corner.

Week 4

WILLEM'S PLASTER CAST CAME OFF HIS FOOT TODAY.

Gracie took me and Willem to celebrate at the All You Can Eat for Five Pounds Chinese buffet in Kentish Town. The manager, Mr Wong, knows Gracie and always lets Willem have a different plate for each dish. We were allowed to sit on the biggest table so he could spread them all out. We ate our five pounds' worth all right.

Willem handed me a letter across the table and a parcel wrapped in brown paper and string.

'What's this, Willem?' I said. 'It ain't my birthday.'

He just smiled.

I opened the letter.

18th Floor
Flat 103 Beckham Estate
Beckham Street
Camden Town
London
NW1 7AD

Dear Sasha,

From the day you rescued me from the hospital, you were my amber friend. This means 'proceed with caution'. This is because I did not know you very well. I had to be sure you would not abandon me or laugh at me. After a lot of thought and consideration I have now decided to make you my green friend. These are the friends that go with me through the days, hours and minutes of my life. Green is my favourite colour and makes me feel safe. I know that you will always go with me and that we are friends for life. Please accept this gift in honour of our friendship.

Your friend

Willem Edward Smith

I ripped the parcel open. Inside was a stunning green scarf with beads.

'I bought it with my pocket money from Camden Market,' said Willem. 'It cost £8.99.'

'Willem,' said Gracie, spluttering on her prawn crackers, 'you don't tell a lady how much a gift cost.'

I felt proper choked.

'That green looks lovely with your dark hair,' said Gracie.

I held my hand out to Willem.

'Green friend,' I said.

'Green friends,' he said and held my hand tight.

Now that Willem's foot was mended he could walk faster to catch up with Finn, to tell him more facts about the Spitfire. HA HA. Finn just runs away.

And as for the Beckham Estate – it's gone quiet. Archie has bewitched people. Those boys just spend all their time stripping engines as part of his Community Project. Of course there is still beef between the Beckham Boyz and T Crew, but they seem to be spending their energy taking apart engines rather than each other. Archie hops and skips around the estate spreading his magic.

TJ spends every waking hour in Archie's garage

and has decided he wants to do this fiddling with engines as a job when he is older. Since TJ's transformation from muppet to mechanic, Aunty Lou thinks Archie is Jesus's right-hand man.

'Archie,' she says, 'I've just brought you a little chicken,' but there's always more than enough for all of us to feed our faces.

At school Mrs Hubert hits me with her beadies at every opportunity.

'Sasha,' she says, 'remember you must redeem yourself at the presentation for running out of school like that without permission. ONLY TWO WEEKS TO GO.'

Willem
Week 5

I was tired. My bones ached. While Sasha and Finn went to Bernie's to get number 3 and 7 meals with extra chips, I had been to our Spitfire Club House to collect a bit more of my secret to make my surprise for the presentation. I do not like surprises, but I like to give them to other people. Gran says that it is a contradiction in my personality and that's what makes me special.

I managed to get my secret up in the lift to the 18th floor to my bedroom in Flat 103 of the Beckham Estate, Beckham Street, North West London, NW1 7AD.

I was sitting on my bed with my eyes shut, so that I could pretend I was in Maisy's cockpit. It is hard to do it with my eyes open because my Bart Simpson duvet cover on my bed gets in the way.

I started reciting the pre-flight checks that I had learned from my 'How to Fly a Spitfire' manual.

Trims	**Rudder fully right**
Throttle fiction	**Tight**

'Willem . . .' Gran interrupted my focus. I squeezed my eyes shut tighter.

Mixture control	**Fully back**

'WILLEM, can you come here, please?'

Propeller Pitch Control	**Fully forward**

'WILLEM!!!!!!'

It is hard to be a Spitfire pilot when your gran is in the kitchen.

I came down to earth and climbed out of the cockpit and went into the kitchen to answer her.

Gran was cooking a chicken casserole with dumplings.

'Oh, there you are,' said Gran. 'Archie is coming here for his tea tonight. On your way down to Maisy's hangar, please can you ring on his bell and tell him supper's ready? I will save some for you for later.'

'Yes, Gran,' I said. I put on a yellow jumper and walked out to the lift.

As I travelled down I held my breath. I do not like the smell of wee. I took my Spitfire out of my pocket and spun the propeller really fast.

The lift stopped at the 11th floor and when the doors opened Laurence and a group of Beckham Street Boyz were outside.

They are all red people. I spun the propeller faster.

A tall boy called Nathan, who has a nose stud and 2 gold teeth, stuck his foot in the door.

'Look who it is. Freak Boy,' he sneered.

He leaned forward. He was too near my face.

'What you got there, Willem, man, your little toy? Ahhh,' he said.

'No, it is not a toy. It is a Spitfire Mark 1,' I told him.

'Miss lets him play with that in Maths,' said Laurence.

'Is that right?' said Nathan, who snatched it out of my hand and threw it to Laurence. I stepped out of the lift and tried to grab my Spitfire, but my fingers were jiggling too much. A boy called Ryan, who is in my Art class, caught it.

'Please,' I said, 'can I have it back? It is not a toy. It is a model Spitfire.'

They kept throwing it and throwing it and I was reaching and reaching, but I could not catch it.

Nathan still had his foot in the door of the lift.

'What's happening here?' said Finn, walking towards us. Throwing his school bag on the floor, he punched his fist in the air and thumped 3 of the fingers of his right hand into the palm of his left, which is their Beckham Street Boyz gang sign.

Laurence grabbed the Spitfire and held it over

the balcony. 'Shall we see if it flies?'

My Spitfire could not fly. It did not have an engine. I ran up to Finn.

'Scramble,' I said, 'scramble.' Which was the secret code for the Spitfire Club to signal that an urgent private conversation was needed.

Finn hesitated, then held out his hand. 'Laurence, give us it. I want to see if it flies myself.'

Laurence shrugged and handed over the Spitfire.

'Now you lot, scoot. I need to talk to Willem here by myself, do you understand me?'

The boys got in the lift and the doors closed on them. I held out my fist to my friend Finn's fist.

Finn looked over the balcony until we saw the boys come out of the lift and walk across the courtyard, towards Bernie's.

Finn handed me back my Spitfire. I checked it was not broken and put it in my pocket.

'Come on,' he said. 'We need to get to the Club House or Sasha will be vexed.' And he offered me a chip from the number 7 meal he had in his school bag.

I took one that was not touching the chicken and my friend and I waited for the lift to come.

Sasha
Week 6

Mrs Hubert reminded us in Maths today that this is our final week before the presentation.

The fear tickled my tummy. Every day after school that week we worked on our presentation, then together with Archie we strived to finish our restorations to Maisy. We checked the pressure in the tyres, did a final check on the flying controls, checked the oils and a million other things that the Spitfire needed. We buffed and puffed and scrubbed Maisy till she looked proper beautiful.

And on the SATURDAY NIGHT WE FINALLY FINISHED, giving the canopy and the windscreen one last clean.

Aunty Lou, Dad, Gracie and Trish were invited into Maisy's hangar and given a glass of Champagne by Archie to celebrate.

They were proper chuffed with us. Dad even said he was proud of me and gave me a hug. I overheard Trish whisper to Archie, 'Thanks for keeping Finn busy and out of trouble. I think this is the first good thing he's achieved in his life.'

We said our goodnights and the Spitfire Club arranged to meet tomorrow, the final day before the presentation to get it proper perfect.

SUNDAY – THE FINAL DAY

I looked at the photograph of Rachel propped up against my dressing table mirror, as I scraped my hair back in a ponytail and put on my best gold hoop earrings. I ran all the way down to Maisy's hangar. As it was Sunday, the garage project lay deserted. It was quiet everywhere.

I knocked and whispered 'Maisy's Rain' – but there was no answer. I opened the door. The hangar was empty, apart from Maisy, of course. As I waited for the boys to come, I noticed there was no wood left in the corner. Maybe Archie had taken it. I looked around – nothing else seemed to have been touched. I sat on Maisy's wing and waited and waited and waited, but no one came.

18

Sasha

Where were they? I couldn't wait a second more. I'd had enough.

I ran back to the estate and up to the eleventh floor. I banged on Finn's door until Trish opened it.

'FINN, SASHA'S HERE,' she yelled as she let me through.

His bedroom door was shut. It sounded as if he was watching something on his stupid computer.

'I'VE BEEN WAITING FOR YOU, FINN MASON. I'M PROPER ANNOYED,' I shouted.

'Got things to do, Sash. I'm reading up about Spitfires,' he said, 'getting ready for the presentation.' It sounded to me as if he was just watching *Battle of Britain* on YouTube.

'But what about the Spitfire Club?' I yelled. 'Finn?'

No answer.

'This is our last practice!'

All I could hear was the drone of Spitfires coming from his computer.

'I am on my last chance, Finn, and you know that,' I shouted. 'I am off to get Willem. We'll do it without you.' And I gave his door a final kick as I left.

As I stomped up to the eighteenth floor, I thought about how Finn had been proper secretive at school all week. I kept catching him whispering in corners with Laurence and TJ, which gave my bones the jitters.

I looked down to the courtyard and I couldn't believe my eyes. There was Finn!

The cheek of the boy, sneaking out as soon as I left. There they were, mini Finn, TJ and Laurence, pointing up to the roof.

They were plotting something, I knew it.

I rang the doorbell and Gracie answered.

'He won't come out of his bedroom, Sasha. You give it a try.'

What was wrong with these boys today!

'Willem – it's me, Sasha. Come on, it's our last rehearsal today,' I called through Willem's door.

'Sasha,' he said, 'you must go away – I am busy.'

'Doing what, Willem?' I shouted.

'It is a secret. But it will make our presentation the best in the class. We will get lots of merit marks.'

I tried to have a peep through the keyhole but he'd stuffed it with cotton wool.

'Willem, you know Mrs Hubert said it was my last chance.'

I put my ear to the door and all I could hear was Willem muttering things. 'Trims . . . Rudder fully right . . . Throttle fiction tight . . .'

'Willem, what are you doing? You sound like you are flying an aeroplane.'

He didn't answer me, so I banged on his door.

'We are meant to be working together.' Bang. 'Come out now. I want words.' Bang. I banged on his door till my hands hurt.

'Sasha, you must go away. I am busy.'

The Spitfire Club was drifting.

I gave up and wandered back through to the kitchen. Archie was sitting at the table with tea and a plate of digestive biscuits. He was often there when I went to knock for Willem. He was probably doing odd jobs for Gracie in his breaks from the garage. I think he liked being on the eighteenth floor – nearer the sky.

'Come on, sit yourself down,' said Gracie, as she put some cheese-on-toast on the table for me.

'What am I going to do? Gracie, the presentation's tomorrow and Finn's down there messing with TJ and Laurence, and Willem won't come out, and the Spitfire Club has broken down.'

I had to quickly banish a tear. I was proper embarrassed 'cause I'm not that soppy.

Archie pulled a chair out for me. His eyes twinkled.

'No matter how hard things were, my mother Rachel would just carry on flying those Spitfires. She ferried the Spitfires and Ansons and other planes from the factories to the airfields in all weathers, and then she would fly another plane back if needed,' said Archie.

And it was like time ticked backwards and I was there.

'Or sometimes she'd get the train back to base and be worried the whole journey about arriving before the blackout, but she always kept a smile on her face. She made the most of every minute of her life. Rachel would go dancing at every opportunity at the Dorchester or the Brevet Club, then back to base on the morning milk train to fly the Spitfires.'

I was there dancing with her. I was there flying the Spitfire. Like magic. It was as if I was Rachel and Rachel was me. I knew that I could make *my bit* of the presentation the best ever.

'Archie, I was wondering . . . umm . . . would it be possible to take Rachel's notes and things in to school tomorrow for my presentation? I promise to guard them with my life.'

'My mother would be honoured that you are doing a presentation about her,' said Archie.

Gracie asked Archie to help her grab a suitcase from the top of the wardrobe. There was a scuffling and a giggle behind the closed bedroom door. Gracie appeared with an old brown suitcase. She was red in the face. The suitcase must have been hard to reach.

We all went down to Archie's in the stinking lift. He switched on the light and we went into his front room. He opened the case on the floor and in it we packed the red dress, the flying hats, Rachel's shoes, and finally he handed me her handbag with the love notes from Robert inside.

I kneeled next to the case; for the first time in my life I was proper speechless. I stroked the silky red dress. I opened the old leather handbag and smelled the scent of face powder from the grains that lingered. I carefully, carefully looked at the notes, then put them back in a pocket inside the bag.

I stood up and flung my arms around Archie.

'Thank you, thank you so much for trusting me with Rachel's treasures,' I mumbled, all choked up.

Gracie gave me a hug.

'You be the best that you can be tomorrow. You show that Mrs Hubert what you are made of.'

But I wasn't doing it for Mrs Hubert. I was doing it for Rachel.

19

WILLEM

It was the day of our presentation. I was going to get lots of merit marks for excellence. I had hidden my secret behind the girls' changing rooms, next to the hole in the fence, which is used as a forbidden shortcut to school. Mr Patricks should mend the hole. It is school rule number 4 that we should walk through the front gate in an orderly manner. I had wrapped my secret in 5 of Gran's extra-strong bin bags. I had sellotaped them together. I hoped that she would not mind. I took them without asking.

Inside the classroom, Mrs Hubert was shouting, 'Settle down, class.' She was trying to get the class to be quiet ready for our Spitfire presentation. No one was listening.

Finn and Sasha walked down the corridor towards me. Finn had his arm round Sasha's shoulder, and she was wheeling my gran's suitcase. Finn was carrying rolls of paper. Sasha had her angry face on and shook his arm off. Finn kept whispering things in her ear. By the time they reached me, they were both laughing.

It was not funny that today was our presentation. My right hand was jiggling. I put it in my pocket so that nobody could see.

'Finn and Sasha,' I said, 'WILL YOU PLEASE STOP LAUGHING AND CONCENTRATE.'

'Keep your hair on, Willem,' said Finn.

'My hair is on my head, Finn,' I said.

Mrs Hubert put her head out of the door.

'We are ready for you,' she said.

'We'll be ready in a tick, Miss,' said Sasha.

'1 MINUTE,' said Mrs Hubert.

'Finn,' I said, 'please do not mumble. Please concentrate until you have said all your facts about Maisy. Do not use any bad words or we will lose merit marks. Sasha, I know that you will do your best to tell the class all about Rachel. If you speak with a clear voice and do not answer Mrs Hubert back, even if she is rude, you will get your redemption.'

'Chocks away,' said Sasha and gave Finn and me a high-5.

'Chocks away,' Finn and I said together.

We walked into the classroom and stood in front of the class. Sasha wheeled in Gran's case and opened it.

The class were shuffling. 3 people were texting under their desks: Ruth Evans, Carrie Dalton and Marie O'Brian.

Finn glared at everyone till they stopped talking. Richie Lane and the T Crew rocked back on their chairs.

Finn unrolled his paper and pinned it to the white board with a magnet. At the top were pictures of the dials in the cockpit of a Spitfire.

Finn glared round the classroom then mumbled, 'If the pilots in World War 2 hadn't been able to read the numbers on the dials, well, they wouldn't have been able to fly the aeroplanes and we wouldn't have won the Battle of Britain, right, so history would have been changed. That's why numbers are vital.'

My class were listening. Finn's voice got clearer.

Underneath the pictures of dials was the story of Maisy. Finn had stuck photographs and his painting of the Spitfire markings. He had told me what he wanted to say. I had labelled everything for him because Finn cannot spell.

Finn spoke with his polite voice. He told the story of Malcolm the millionnaire dying and leaving Maisy to the person who could claim a connection with the Spitfire; how that was Archie, because his mother Rachel had been a Spitfire pilot in World War 2. Finn's voice got louder. He explained about the garage project and he pointed to the photographs of the renovation that we had done to Maisy.

He pointed to a photograph of the inlet and exhaust valves we had replaced.

He showed a picture of Sasha replacing a part of the wing that was corroded.

He showed a picture of me working on one of the radiator flaps so that it would open with ease.

The last picture was of the Spitfire Club, with Buster and Archie standing on Maisy's wing, waving our arms in the air.

Everyone was listening apart from Carrie, Ruth

and Marie, who were still texting. Richie Lane had stopped rocking on his chair. Mrs Hubert had her happy face on.

Then Sasha stepped forwards and I now understand the saying *she had fire in her eyes*. Sasha looked very beautiful. She held the dress up and spoke of Rachel dancing in the clouds in the day with the Spitfire and at night in the red dress.

She held up Rachel and Robert's notes for the class to see and then read out loud the notes from Robert.

Rachel, my angel of the sky,
Will you marry me?

Carrie, Ruth and Marie stopped texting. I think Mrs Hubert had something in her eye, as she had a happy face on but a tear trickled down her cheek.

Then everyone started to clap and the clapping got louder and louder and louder.

'WAIT,' I shouted. 'PLEASE WAIT, we have not finished yet.'

I ran out of the door and across the playground, and round to the back of the girls' changing rooms and dragged my secret back all the way to the classroom.

It was 2 minutes till the end of the lesson. People

were packing their bags and walking out of the door.

'STOP,' I shouted. 'WE HAVE NOT FINISHED. PLEASE. I HAVE A SECRET. PLEASE LISTEN.'

'Quiet everyone and sit down. Willem has something to say,' shouted Mrs Hubert.

And I ripped open the bin bags and revealed my secret.

MY WOODEN WINGS.

They were a copy of the flying machine that was created by the painter and inventor, Mr Leonardo da Vinci. I had adapted the wings and design to my own dimensions.

There was silence. No one said a single word. My class were listening to me.

I read a quote from Mr J. M. Barrie, who is the gentleman who wrote *Peter Pan*.

'*The reason birds can fly and we can't is simply because they have perfect faith, for to have faith is to have wings* . . . One day I am going to fly,' I said, and everyone started to laugh. 'Please stop – it is not a joke. I AM GOING TO FLY.'

Everyone laughed louder. 'PLEASE,' I said, 'YOU NEED TO BE QUIET SO I CAN EXPLAIN THE

EQUATIONS I USED TO BUILD MY WINGS.'

But my class would not listen and laughed louder.

Sasha stretched out her arm and we stood there, wing tip to wing tip, in front of the screeching, laughing class.

Finn smiled a horrible smile, like the one he did when he used to make me jump off things. He nodded to TJ and Laurence. Finn punched his fist in the air and thumped 3 of the fingers of his right hand into the palm of his left. The Beckham Street Boyz secret gang sign.

They did not think I saw but I did.

20

WILLEM

The bell rang for afternoon break. Finn was waiting for me in the playground. He put his fist to my fist.

'Nice one, Willem,' he said. 'So you think you can fly?'

'Yes,' I said. 'Why are you talking to me? I saw you laughing at me with the others. You do not usually talk to me at school. You only talk to me at the Spitfire Club. I am trying to make you my green friend, but you do not want to know me.'

'What are you talking about?' said Finn. 'Green friend? I ain't green.'

So I told him in quick words about my homework from Mrs Hubert.

A smile spread slowly over Finn's face.

'I know a way that you can have lots of friends,

do ya hear me? Get tons of merit marks for that Headteacher's Cup of Excellency thingy. How'd you like to be in the Beckham Street Boyz? But you have to do an initiation test first.'

'I am good at tests,' I said. 'What do I have to do?'

Finn whispered in my ear.

Sasha

We'd done it! My emotions were having a boxing match in my tummy. Parts of our presentation were proper brilliant. I know I'd done Rachel proud. Even Finn had done OK. But then it had ended in proper mayhem 'cause of Willem and his wings – and my doubt won.

Mrs Hubert asked to see me at afternoon break.

'Please,' I said over and over again inside my head, as I made my way to the staff room. 'Please let Mrs Hubert count my bit of the presentation and let me off my last chance.'

I knocked on the door. When Mrs Hubert opened it, I could see all the teachers drinking, laughing and talking about us through the crack in the door.

Mrs Hubert was munching on a chocolate Hobnob. She had crumbs stuck on her teeth.

'Please, Miss,' I said, 'PLEASE. We worked really hard. I know it turned chaotic but—'

'Sasha, CALM YOURSELF, PLEASE,' she said. 'You were truly excellent today.'

Relief filled me from head to toe.

'And I was also impressed with the way you stood by Willem, when the class were laughing,' she coughed. 'Willem does not always understand what is going on.'

'He understands a lot of other things though, Miss,' I said. 'And of course I stuck by him, that is what friends do.'

'Yes, quite,' said Mrs Hubert.

'Am I redeemed, Miss?' I decided not to chance my luck by asking about merit marks.

'Almost,' said Mrs Hubert, 'almost . . . Mr Hudson,' she called over her shoulder to the coffee-guzzling music teacher. 'You were after someone to tidy up the music cupboard, weren't you, Mr Hudson?'

'Ah, Sasha,' he said, coming to the door. 'The perfect candidate, what with your musical background.'

'If you do this for Mr Hudson after school, we will

say no more about your punishment for running out of school,' said Mrs Hubert.

My gob hung open in proper disbelief. Just 'cause my dad was in a wrinkly band doesn't make me suitable for cleaning up a lot of dusty old xylophones and triangles. Where's the logic?

I got the jitters in my tummy. Every bit of my instinct was telling me to stick by Willem's side, 'cause I had seen Finn's smile and the gang signal. I had seen it.

'Please, Mr Hudson. I need to get home tonight. I will do it tomorrow, PLEASE.'

'Sasha Barton, you will do as you are told. TONIGHT,' said Mr Hudson.

My gut punched the floor.

I tried to sort out the jumble of guitar and amp leads and pedals and my nerves were getting tangled. I wanted to check on Willem.

I sorted the triangles from the tambourines and the drums and put them in separate plastic boxes, all tidy. When I was finished I ran down the corridor to my locker. There was a note stuck on the door.

Dear Sasha,
I would like to invite you on to the roof of the Beckham Estate.
It is important that you attend. I have something to show you.
It is a secret.
Your friend,
Willem Edward Smith

The jitters in my tummy jumped up into my brain.
Something bad was going to happen, I knew it. I ripped
the note off the locker, opened it and grabbed my
school bag and ran down the corridor, burst through
the swing doors, and across the playground, falling
flat on my face. No time for pain. I dragged myself up
and ran on my stinging knees round the back of the
girls' changing room and through the forbidden gap
in the fence.

Willem

I hoped that God was listening – or his assistant, St Peter. I sent a prayer that Sasha would get the note that I had stuck on her locker.

My muddy trainers left footprints on the newly washed floor – proof that I had existed, just in case anything should go wrong with my initiation test. JUST IN CASE. But, according to my calculations, I would fly.

Grabbing my school bag, I eased out my pencil box from its place between Physics Advanced Book 3 and my atlas. I tore a page out of my Maths exercise book and wrote a note. Gran would expect me to be waiting with the teapot for her when she got back from the 65 Club. She would not be expecting me to be taking part in a gang initiation ceremony.

I wrote her a note with my new gel pen.

Dear Gran,

I am sorry that I will not be here to make your cup of tea and give you a digestive biscuit when you come home. I have gone to make some friends.

Your grandson,

Willem Edward Smith

I stuck the note to the fridge, next to my poem *Sounds in my Head*, with her *A Gift from Blackpool* fridge magnet. I left a trail from the kitchen table to the fridge, with my new rubber, my protractor, compass and gel pens, leaving the green one (my favourite) till last, so that Gran would see my note. I pushed my key through the letterbox as a precaution – in case it fell out of my pocket when I was airborne. I did not want Gran to worry and think the key had gone as well as her only grandson, Willem Edward Smith.

I picked up my wooden Leonardo wings leaning against the wall and started to walk along the balcony. Through the half-open doors, and the lift shaft, and the stairwell, came the chant 'Fly, boy, fly' – whispered then screamed. I shut my eyes and counted to 10.

I pushed open the fire door and dragged my wings on to the roof. There was a good wind blowing.

Finn was waiting, giving a nod of his head. Laurence and TJ stepped out of the shadows, grabbed my wrists and tied on my wooden wings. TJ was shaking as he did it. I do not think he thought I could fly.

'TJ, do not be afraid,' I said. 'I can fly.'

Finn punched him in the stomach. More and more kids from Archie's garage project crowded on to the roof. I could not see Sasha. I looked and looked. 'Sasha,' I called. 'SASHA.'

She was not there.

They walked me over to the south side of the roof, above the side of the flats. There was a good wind behind me, blowing from a north-easterly direction.

The Beckham Street Boyz and T Crew crowded round me, pushing me nearer and nearer to the edge. I could feel something wet and warm trickling down my leg.

The wind dropped. The air was still. I knew I would not fly without wind.

'Scramble,' I said to Finn. 'Scramble.'

Finn ignored me.

'SCRAMBLE, SCRAMBLE, SCRAMBLE,' I cried.

'JUMP!' screamed Finn.

'JUMP! JUMP! JUMP! JUMP!' shouted both the gangs.

There was a gust of wind. I stretched my wooden wings.

I was flying.

Sasha

I ran across the courtyard and over to Archie's project, tripping smack over a proper annoying, yattering crow that hopped right in my path then flapped into the sky joining the rest of the birds as they sang a warning song.

There was a note stuck on the shutter.

Back in one hour. Archie

The project was deserted. I ran round to the lift. I needed to get to the roof. NOW. Malisha and Tamsin stepped out of the stairwell.

'MOVE,' I shouted.

Tamsin ripped my school bag from my shoulder and threw it on the floor. Malisha grabbed my hair.

'Think you're something, don't you? Singing on stage, having your picture in the paper with that old black-and-white days plane.'

'Let go, Malisha. I NEED TO GO,' I screamed.

Tamsin grabbed my other arm.

'You're not going anywhere,' she spat. 'YOU ARE GOING TO WATCH.'

And with that, they dragged me backwards round to the side of the flats. I struggled and kicked but Malisha pulled my hair back till I was watching the roof, and then let go.

And he was in the air. My Willem. And the wind caught his wings and for a second my strange, special friend was flying.

Willem

UP.

up

up

I was flying up

But then I started to drop

down

down

down.

Sasha

He was falling.

'NOOOOOOOOOOO!' I heard a howl from the middle of the Earth. And I realized it was coming from me and the birds stopped singing.

Willem

Then I stopped, my wings splintering, flapping in the wind.

Sasha

His wings had caught — they had caught round a satellite dish. It was in front of Finn's window. It was Finn's satellite dish! My scream got louder, filling my world.

Willem

I do not like being higher than the birds. I looked up, with 1 broken wing caught round a satellite dish and the other wedged behind a pipe. My body dangled in the air. The tip of my wing splintered. As I dropped approximately 30.48 centimetres, my body spun round and I was facing the flats. I could see an untidy bedroom through a gap in the curtains. There were photographs and a painting of Maisy strewn across the carpet. IT MUST BE FINN'S BEDROOM! He had not made his bed. I tried to flap my wings. My wings splintered again. I slipped down approximately 4 centimetres. I did not fall, but a bit of my wing fell down into the courtyard of the Beckham Estate. And then I slipped down again.

'HELP,' I cried. 'PLEASE HELP, I DO NOT WANT TO DIE.'

I tried to flap my broken wings again.

'Willem, keep still!' Sasha's tiny words were carried to me on the breeze.

'Sasha,' I shouted. 'Sasha, did you see?' I flew for 17.3 seconds. Don't leave me!' I do not know if she heard me.

Sasha

'STAY THERE,' I shouted, which was a proper stupid thing to say, 'cause where did I think he was going to go? I pulled myself together; I needed to call for help. WHERE WAS MY PHONE? I looked for my bag. It had gone!

'WHERE'S MY BAG?' I screamed at Malisha. 'We need to phone for the fire brigade or someone to get him down.'

Then feet thundered down the stairs. Malisha and Tamsin laughed and melted into the boys, pushing and shoving. I got thrown backwards and forwards.

'PLEASE, SOMEONE HELP WILLEM,' I cried.

But all the Beckham Street Boyz and T Crew stood,

heads back, mouths open, gaping at Willem – waiting for my friend to fall.

'SOMEONE HELP HIM,' I cried. 'I've got no phone. Call the fire brigade. *SOMEONE!*' No one listened.

He slipped again. Bits of his broken wings came crashing down. I opened my mouth. There wasn't a sound. My screams had flown away with the birds.

Then windows slamming up, doors banging open, people's heads popping out shouting, 'WHAT ARE YOU LOT DOING?'

'YOU GOING TO RIOT AGAIN?'

'NO MORE TROUBLE!'

Someone threw a shoe.

'GO ON, SCOOT.'

'PLEASE,' I shouted, 'Willem – he tried to fly. HELP!'

But no one heard me.

'Cause those people, THEY COULDN'T SEE WILLEM. If they had only stuck their heads out backwards and looked up. They would have seen my friend with broken wings. They just saw a gathering of gangs.

'I'M CALLING THE POLICE IF YOU LOT DON'T

MOVE,' shouted Tamsin's mum from the second-floor balcony.

Then someone grabbed my wrist with a cold, hard grip. It was Finn.

'Finn, please – you've got to help Willem.'

A distant police siren shattered the air. In my muddled brain I thought someone had called and help was on its way.

'RUN,' shouted Finn. 'RUN.'

Rachel danced into my head. She smiled at me, sending me pure strength. I had run from Willem once. I would not run again.

'No,' I said.

'What?' said Finn.

'I said NO. Get off me, Finn. I know that you're behind this, with your secret smiles and stupid signs. HELP HIM.'

'He said he could fly,' said Finn.

'FOOL,' I screamed. 'I HATE YOU.'

The police siren got louder.

'Sasha, RUN,' shouted Finn.

'No! Willem thinks you're his friend. I will not run with you. If he falls he will have me holding him, whether he's alive or dead. SO YOU GO BACK TO YOUR

FLAT AND HELP HIM 'cause we are the Spitfire Club.'

The police siren screeched round the corner. Finn let go of my wrist and ran. I sank to the floor. The jitters took me over, but I forced my head up to look at my special friend caught creaking in the breeze and cried, 'WILLEM, I'M HERE – I'M NOT LEAVING YOU.'

The siren got nearer and nearer and nearer and then drove right past.

'HELP,' I cried. 'COME BACK!'

But there was just silence and no birds sang.

A car drove into the courtyard. A door opened and Gracie stuck her leg out and Archie rushed round to help her out of the car.

'WILLEM,' I shouted, 'YOUR GRAN'S HERE,' and I dragged myself up and I ran, ran, ran as fast as I could towards Gracie and Archie.

21

WILLEM

I said a prayer to God: 'Please help me.' A bit more of the right wing splintered and disappeared down into the courtyard of the Beckham Estate. God must be busy.

So I said a prayer to his assistant.

'St Peter, will you help me?'

Finn ran into his bedroom and up to the window. His face was white. His body was shaking. He stared at me hanging there. My wings broken.

'FINN,' I shouted. 'FINN, HELP ME. I DO NOT WANT TO DIE.'

Finn opened the window.

'Willem, you're not going to die. I'm going to grab you, OK?'

As he reached out to try to hold my hand, the

door was kicked open and Finn's dad, who is called Craig, staggered in. He was drinking out of a bottle.

'I've been shouting for you. Where have you been?'

He dragged Finn away from the window. I don't think his eyes saw me.

'Acting the hard man, have you, with your little friends? I wanted you to get me a paper from the shop. What happens when you don't do as I say?'

Finn locked eyes with me, his face bright red.

'I have to jump,' stammered Finn.

'Louder, I can't hear you.'

'I HAVE TO JUMP,' screamed Finn.

'GET ON THE BED,' shouted Finn's dad.

Finn climbed on the bed.

'WHEN I ORDER YOU TO JUMP, YOU JUMP, DO YOU UNDERSTAND?'

Finn nodded.

'Jump,' shouted Craig into Finn's face. 'JUMP.'

Finn jumped.

Then Craig made him climb on to the chest of drawers. 'JUMP,' he shouted.

Finn jumped off. He was crying.

Craig started laughing and then staggered out. I

heard the front door bang. My wings splintered again.

'FINN, HELP!' I shouted.

Finn ran to the window.

'SWING,' he yelled. 'Swing your legs to me.'

I tried, but my wings splintered some more and I dropped approximately 2 centimetres.

I could hear screams.

Finn leaned out. He looked down. His face went pale. He climbed on to the windowsill. His legs were shaking. 'Try again,' he said.

I could hear gasps. I peeped down. Crowds of people looking up, watching my broken wings.

'1, 2, 3 . . .' said Finn.

I used all of my strength and Finn caught my legs and he fell backwards through the window, holding on to me. My foot kicked him in the mouth. My legs were inside his bedroom but my arms would not go through because of my broken wings, so I started to fall backwards. Finn reached out and snapped my wings in half, and bits flew down to the courtyard. He then pulled me to safety. Finn saved my life.

We stood and stared at each other. No words

came. Finn's lip had a bit of blood on it.

Then he looked at the wet patch on my school trousers and I felt ashamed.

'Here.' He threw me some jeans. 'Put these on.'

I do not like wearing other people's clothes but I do not like wearing wet trousers so I put them on.

Finn and I stared at each other again.

'You do not like to jump either,' I said.

Finn said no words.

'I said "scramble",' I said, 'but you did not have an urgent private conversation with me.'

Finn looked at the carpet.

Mrs Hubert said it is important to make eye contact when forming friendships.

Finn still said no words.

'I flew for 17.3 seconds. Are you my friend now?' I asked.

Sirens screeching, hurting my ears.

I looked out of the window.

Police everywhere, running, rounding up the kids who had wanted to see me fly.

Finn stood next to me and watched. He was shivering.

Then my legs went wobbly and I sank to the floor.

More sirens.

Footsteps outside.

Banging on the door.

'This is the police. Finn Mason, I know you are in there. Open up.'

Finn scurried out of his bedroom.

I crawled under the bed to make the noise stop.

Finn does not tidy under his bed. There was 1 magazine, 1 broken weight from a gym, 7 paperclips and 3 unopened letters from the school that were hidden under a piece of carpet.

I curled up in a ball and shut out the planet. Something wet and warm brushed my cheek.

It was Buster, giving me a dog kiss. He was shaking. I buried my face in his fur, and my green friend and I hid under the bed, waiting.

22

WILLEM

I could hear a lot of bad noise from under the bed. Doors banging, voices of strangers shouting.

Buster growled. He did not like bad noise either.

I put my arm round my friend Buster, who was snuggling next to me in our hiding place under the bed.

'It is all right, Buster,' I said. This was a lie.

I closed my eyes and recited an aeroplane fact. 'In an emergency situation when a pilot has to land soon after take off, the pilot might choose to eject fuel from the wings.' I heard the door open and my gran's voice. 'Willem?'

'I am here,' I said, crawling out from under the bed. 'It is me – your grandson, Willem Edward Smith.'

'Willem,' said Gran, 'my Willem' and hugged me, even though she knows I do not like being hugged. The hug hurt. Gran had tears pouring down her face. I had not seen my gran cry before.

'I flew, Gran,' I said, 'for 17.3 seconds I flew.'

'Willem, you could have been killed,' she said.

I saw Finn through the door – Archie had his hand on Finn's shoulder and was talking to a policeman by the kitchen at the end of the corridor.

A policewoman came into Finn's room to speak to me. 'I am PC Alice Brown and that is PC Luke Turnball,' she said, nodding to the policeman talking to Finn. 'I think you should be sitting down, Willem.'

My legs did feel wobbly so I sat on Finn's bed.

Buster jumped up at PC Alice Brown.

'Good boy,' she said. 'Sit. Come on, sit.'

Buster ignored her and got up on his hind legs, doing his dog dance and howling.

'BUSTER,' said Gran. 'SHUSH.' She sat next to me on Finn's bed.

Buster climbed on her lap.

PC Alice leaned out of the window to look where

my broken wings had got caught around the satellite dish.

'We are rounding up all the boys that we know or suspect were on the roof,' she said.

'They came to watch me fly,' I said. 'You missed it.'

The policewoman looked at me like I was a mad person. I do not think she believed that I flew for 17.3 seconds.

Sasha ran into the bedroom with Fox.

'*Willem*,' she said, flinging her arms round me. My nose was squashed.

'You talked to me from the ground when my wings were broken. I heard you,' I said.

'I thought you were going to die,' said Sasha.

'Give him some air, Sash,' said Fox. 'I'll leave you with your friend. I'll just be out there if you need me.'

'Scramble,' whispered Sasha, in my ear. 'Scramble.' This meant it was time for the Spitfire Club to have an urgent and private discussion. This meant we needed Finn, but I knew that the police would not let me speak to Finn. I have studied police documentaries.

'I am going to go to the kitchen to get a glass of water,' I said.

'No, I'll get one brought in for you,' said PC Alice.

I started to cough and splutter and my hand started to jiggle.

Gran was rubbing my back.

'He's got himself into one of his states,' said Sasha. 'I'll have to go with him, Miss. I'm the only one who can snap him out of it. He has to choose his own drinking glass. Willem's proper particular.'

'Let them go,' said Gran. 'Sasha will keep an eye on him.'

As soon as we left Finn's bedroom, I stopped coughing and smiled at Sasha.

'Willem,' she whispered, giggling, 'you faker.'

'I was doing acting,' I said.

She winked at me.

I think one day I would like to kiss Sasha.

'Come on,' she said. 'Quick!'

We walked down the hall. Buster, the 4th member of the Spitfire Club, followed us. The kitchen door was ajar.

Finn was sitting in the corner on the floor, his

225

back against the wall. He was shaking and crying. His lip was bleeding.

Footsteps.

Sasha pulled me into the bathroom just in time. We peeped through a gap in the door. PC Turnball came out of the kitchen and walked past, talking on his radio. He opened the front door. I could see Archie and Fox talking on the balcony.

'Hurry,' said Sasha, and we darted out of the bathroom and into the kitchen. Buster ran up to Finn, whining and trying to lick his nose. I filled a glass up with water and sat down at the kitchen table to listen to what urgent things Sasha had to say.

A note from Sasha

Finn turned his face away from us.

'Look at me, Finn,' I said.

Finn turned to face me and I saw his nose was running.

'Finn, you nearly killed Willem! Why, Finn? Why? Just tell me.'

Finn's eyes sparked. ''Cause he's always with you,

that's why. You sit next to him in class. You give him little kisses. I thought I was losing you,' hissed Finn.

I COULD NOT BELIEVE WHAT I WAS HEARING.

FINN WAS JEALOUS OF WILLEM.

Willem was trying to sip his water, but his shaking hand was splashing it all over the table. He looked proper confused. My anger kicked in.

'Well maybe, just maybe, I sit with him because he is my friend and he spends time with me and I trust him. He doesn't spend half his life running round with the Beckham Street Boyz. And, Finn, do you honestly think I would ever have talked to you again if Willem had got smashed up?'

I couldn't look at Finn any more so I walked out of the kitchen.

'Come back,' shouted Willem.

I felt a hand in mine. Willem led me back into the kitchen and grabbed hold of Finn's hand.

'Please,' he said, 'we are the Spitfire Club.'

I couldn't look at Finn so I mumbled, 'You saved him and I thank you for that.'

'Sash, take Buster. They are going to take me down to the police station in a bit,' said Finn.

I nodded, but still couldn't look at him.

PC Turnball marched back in and told us off for being in the kitchen. He had a little chat with me about Willem and his broken wings.

The paramedics arrived and checked the boys over. Willem had a right nasty scrape on his back and a cut elbow and a bruised shoulder. BUT THAT'S IT! A proper miracle, if you ask me. It got chaotic and a bit much for Willem. He rolled into a ball and started rocking.

'Willem,' I said, 'don't you lose it now. You've been proper brave and brilliant.'

The paramedics sorted out Finn's cut lip and then Finn was officially arrested. And somewhere in the middle of all that, Trish came back. When she heard what had happened it was like her face split in two; she completely crumpled. Dad held her tight as she sobbed.

The policeman let Finn say goodbye to Buster. He buried his head in Buster's fur and held him tight for the longest time, but then they took Finn away. Buster cried and tried to go after him as they led Finn out of the door, so I put his lead on and gave him a dog treat.

Finn turned back. 'I'm sorry, Willem,' he said. 'Gracie, I didn't mean—'

'Finn, I can't deal with you now. I'm sorry, just go,' said Gracie. Archie stood next to her with his hand on her arm.

Then they took my Finn away from me, on a path I would not follow.

'I need some air,' said Gracie, and went and stood outside the open front door.

I followed her with Buster and looked over the balcony as Finn and Trish walked out into the courtyard, got in the police car and were driven away.

23

Sasha

It was two things that dragged me from my nightmare of Willem falling, falling, falling.

One: the smell of frying bacon and . . .

Two: dog snoring.

Buster had somehow got into my bed and nicked most of the quilt and the pillows. While I, Sasha, whose bed it was the last time I looked, was about to fall off the edge on to the floor.

I gave Buster a dog cuddle and he woke up and licked my nose. I buried my face in his fur. Buster smelled of Finn and my tummy lurched at the thought of him spending a night in a police cell. He'd nearly killed Willem – then saved his life. My feelings toppled over and over each other. But I knew for proper certain that Finn had no control over me any more, NOT EVER AGAIN.

I crossed my fingers that Finn was OK. I then rolled over and looked at my phone. It was ten o'clock. AHHHHH. Late for school. I WAS GOING TO BE IN FOR IT.

I jumped out of bed, getting my foot caught in the quilt and ending up in a heap on the floor with Buster.

'WHY DIDN'T YOU WAKE ME, DAD?' I yelled as I ran into the kitchen with Buster following. I looked around and thought I was still dreaming. The pile of *Gig Weekly* magazines had gone from the table. It was all laid out and Dad was at the stove frying bacon, eggs, mushroom and tomatoes.

'Sasha, chill out. You're not going to school. I've phoned them. Yesterday you saw your friend fly off the roof. This is definitely a Stay in PJs day. You and I are going to have some time.'

And we did, and it was pure magic. After we ate a proper cooked breakfast, Dad and I curled up together on the sofa, with Buster in the middle of us, looking at old photos of mum holding my hand and of Zebra Blue on tour, with me as a tiny baby asleep in the dressing room. I skipped quickly over some photographs of Ferret the drummer. I didn't want to make Dad sad.

Then Dad played the guitar and I sang and Buster howled along and Dad hugged me. He hugged me and hugged me and hugged me and I never wanted this day to end.

Later that day, the doorbell rang. Buster barked and scampered down the hall. It was Archie and Willem.

'You should be dressed,' said Willem. 'It is not bed time. I was not allowed to go to school. I have missed my Maths test.'

'Willem,' said Archie, 'there are more important things in life than Maths tests. Sasha, my dear, if you would like to get ready . . .'

'Ready for what?' I asked.

'You'll see,' said Archie, tapping the end of his nose. 'I will meet you and Willem on the wasteland outside Maisy's hangar in forty-five minutes.'

Despite Buster's best efforts to make me late (tripping me up, jumping in the shower with me, then running round with my jumper in his mouth), forty-five minutes later we were standing outside the Club House. Maisy had been pushed outside and was sitting on the wasteland, sparkling.

Archie handed us the flying hats, but his eyes were not twinkling.

'Willem, you could have died yesterday,' he said. 'Friends do not make you do dangerous things, do you understand me? They are not your friends.'

'Even Finn?' said Willem.

'Even Finn,' said Archie.

'I don't think he understands about friendship,' I said. 'Sometimes I don't understand about friendship. Especially with Finn.'

'We are going for a ride in Maisy. This is how you fly, not with a pair of wooden wings strapped to you. DO YOU UNDERSTAND, WILLEM?'

'Yes, Archie,' said Willem, and he looked proper humble just for a second.

Then his lips twitched and the biggest smile ever creeped across his face and we whirled around with our arms stretched out, laughing.

WE WERE GOING TO FLY.

There was the sound of stamping feet and Mrs Hubert and Mr Richardson appeared from around the corner, marching the Beckham Street Boyz and T Crew from our school towards us. Police vans pulled up and drove over the scrubby wasteland grass. The kids that the police had rounded up, including TJ and Laurence, piled out.

Archie stood on Maisy's wing. He held out his hand and pulled me and Willem to stand next to him. I could see Finn climbing out of a police car that had pulled up behind the others. PC Turnball marched him to stand at the front of the group of boys, and hissed, 'You listen to Archie,' and stood next to him, holding on to his arm. I glued eyes with Finn for a minute then there was a disturbance in the crowd as PC Alice marched Malisha and Tamsin through the boys, to stand next to Finn.

There was silence. Archie glared at the gangs with Pure Anger.

'You nearly killed Willem yesterday. You would have had a death on your hands. Do you all understand me?'

'I did not grass,' said Willem to the crowd. 'Archie said I was helping him with his enquiries.'

I stretched out my arm and we stood there, wing tip to wing tip, facing the gangs.

'Willem thought he could fly,' said Archie, 'with a pair of wooden wings – and none of you stopped him. NOT ONE OF YOU – and you forced Sasha to watch.

You encouraged him and bullied him with your shouts of "Jump, jump, jump". The pack mentality is a dangerous thing. We will probably never know the names of everyone who was there, but those of you who were will have to live with that for the rest of your lives. Now Willem and Sasha are going to really fly.'

There was a silence, so quiet you could hear a robin's song and a crow's hawking. Then TJ started to clap – and one by one the boys joined in. I gave a little wave to Malisha and Tamsin – they scowled back.

Willem climbed down into Maisy's back seat and I climbed in behind him. It was a very close fit. Archie strapped us in. My tummy was turning proper somersaults. I looked through the canopy; Dad was standing with Buster and Gracie at the edge of the courtyard, waving. Willem leaned forward and started shouting out this drill with Archie, like he had been doing it all his life.

Willem:	Archie:
Trims	*Rudder fully right*
Throttle friction	*Tight*

My legs were tingling, my tummy cartwheeling.

Mixture control	*Fully back*
Propeller Pitch Control	*Fully forward*

And on they went . . . and as Archie's hands flew over the levers and buttons they became Rachel's hands, and I could feel her heartbeat and see her strapping herself in, sitting on her parachute ready for take off.

Radiator Flaps	*Open*
Gyros	*Direction indicator*
	synchronized, uncaged
	Artificial horizon erect

The tingling rose up from my toes to the top of my head and my mouth stretched into this gigantic smile.

Hood	*As required*

'Harness,' shouted Archie

'Tight and locked,' we shouted back.

'Chocks away,' bellowed Archie, and Finn stepped forward and moved the wooden blocks from in front of Maisy's wheels. And the crowd stepped back.

Maisy came to life, breathing smoke from her

exhausts. Archie steered her across the wasteland – and we were off. My smile stretched across the world as my cheeks blew back and my eyes watered, and I couldn't help it but I got all choked up when I saw the pure beauty of the Beckham Estate from the sky, as it became a cereal box, then a matchbox, and we dipped and dived and waved at the ant people. Then we were over the willow and oak trees on the Heath and we danced with the clouds, 'cause we had wings, and Rachel held out her hand to me and we skipped back through the years, and a strength pounded through me. It was all I ever dreamed of – only so much better.

Then we dipped and dived and gradually came back to Planet Earth – only nothing in my world would ever, ever, be the same again, 'cause I had wings . . . And as I unsnapped my harness I could see Rachel, her dark hair blowing in the breeze as she took her flying hat off and climbed down from Maisy, running into Robert's arms.

As I climbed out of the cockpit on to Maisy's wing, Archie, who was ahead of me, turned and smiled. A smile that froze as he stumbled and fell against Maisy.

'WILLEM,' I screamed, 'GET YOUR GRAN NOW! RUN AND PHONE FOR THE AMBULANCE.'

Willem jumped out of Maisy and ran.

'Archie,' I said, helping him upright, 'I'm taking you home.' Archie nodded. And the dancing, jigging man leaned against me and shuffled slowly, slowly, to Number One. He gave me his key.

I helped magic man Archie into his room and helped him sit on the end of the bed. I eased his shiny, shiny shoes off his red-socked feet and slowly, slowly swung his legs round on to the bed.

The bedroom door swung open; Gracie and Willem came in.

'What's this, old man?' said Gracie. 'We can't have this, can we?' And she sat on the end of the bed and held his hand.

'The ambulance is coming,' said Willem. 'I dialled nine-nine-nine.'

Archie twinkled at us, but the twinkle started to fade.

'I think my work here is nearly done, my dears,' said Archie.

'Stuff and nonsense, old man,' said Gracie.

We all sat round Archie, counting the minutes until the ambulance came.

When the paramedics arrived I grabbed hold of

one of Willem's hands and squeezed it tight as they tended to him. Then they took magic man Archie away in the ambulance.

24

WILLEM

Finn's new address is:

Maple Park Children's Secure Unit
10 Runcorn Lane
Hertfordshire
SG13 8LC

Archie's new address is:

Bed 6, the one by the window,
Gladstone Ward,
12th floor, Parliament Hill Hospital,
Hampstead
NW3 2PQ

He *was* in bed 4, but I told Nurse Nancy, 'You must move him. Archie needs to see the sky and the clouds to get better.'

So Nurse Nancy moved him. I would not like to sleep in a strange bed that other people had slept in.

Gran does not go to the 65 Club any more. She goes to visit Archie. She went Wednesday, Thursday and Friday. On Saturday Sasha and I came too, but Nurse Nancy said he can only have 2 visitors at a time, so we took it in turns to sit by his bed.

Gran said that I must not go round to the other beds on Archie's ward and read out loud the medical notes on the clipboard at the end of the beds.

'Gran, I thought I was being helpful,' I said.

'YOU ARE NOT,' said Gran. 'Some things are private.'

On Sunday Gran told me to stay at home to do my Science homework, while she went to the hospital.

'Is that so you can talk about the old days?'

'Yes,' she said. 'But you can come with me on Monday evening.'

* * *

It was Monday.

'Are you ready?' said Gran. 'Quick sharp.'

But just as we were about to leave, the doorbell rang. It was Mrs Hubert.

'Is your Gran in, Willem?' she asked.

'Mrs Hubert,' I said, 'you should be at school. This is my home. You must go. We are going to the hospital.'

'Don't be rude, Willem,' said Gran, and she showed Mrs Hubert into the front room. She sat in my gran's best armchair.

My fingers jiggled.

'What can I do for you, Mrs Hubert? Willem hasn't been misbehaving, I hope?'

Mrs Hubert took my 2 letters out of her 'A bag is for life' carrier bag.

The 1st one was the letter I had slipped on her desk, asking Mrs Hubert if I had completed my homework. The 2nd one I had put on her desk after the Spitfire presentation. She showed them to Gran. 'They were buried under a pile of exercise books on my desk. I've only just seen them,' she said.

'You should keep your desk tidy, Mrs Hubert.'

'Willem,' said Gran, in what she calls her warning voice.

Gran read the 2nd letter out loud.

18th Floor
Flat 103 Beckham Estate
Beckham Street
Camden Town
London
NW1 7AD

Dear Mrs Hubert,

You have not yet replied to my letter, where I shared my concerns as to whether my homework was completed.

I wish to inform you that Finn has told me that if I show him I can fly, then I will have lots of friends.

This means that I will definitely have made more than 2 friends of my own age.

(May I have extra merit marks for making more than 2 friends, please? I would like to be a contender for the Headmaster's Cup for Excellency.)

I hope that you enjoyed our Spitfire presentation. We worked very hard indeed. I do hope that you will show a generosity of spirit when distributing merit marks to Sasha, and also to Finn, my friend to be.

I look forward to hearing from you.

Your pupil,

Willem Edward Smith

Gran pursed her lips.

'I feel very much to blame,' said Mrs Hubert. 'I realize that making friends should come naturally. I should never have forced the issue. He could have been killed.'

'Yes,' said Gran, 'he could have. Willem takes things very literally, as you know, Mrs Hubert.'

'Yes, I realize that. I'm so sorry,' she said.

'But have I done my homework, Mrs Hubert? I cannot prove to you that he is my friend now because the judge sent him to a secure unit. He has to stay there till his next court appearance.'

'Willem, how many times? Those boys asking you to fly are not your friends,' said Gran. 'Finn Mason is not your friend. See what trouble your homework has caused, Mrs Hubert?'

'But if I had flown I would have been in the Beckham Street Boyz and then I would have had lots of friends, but I crashed and they ran away,' I pointed out.

'ENOUGH, WILLEM! We don't have gangs in this house,' said Gran.

'But Finn came back and saved me,' I argued.

'Even so,' said Mrs Hubert, and her mouth went

down at the corners.

'Mrs Hubert, don't be sad,' I said. 'If you had not given me that homework I would not be friends with Sasha. My life is happier now. Finn is my sometimes friend. Sasha is my green always friend.'

'There you are, Mrs Hubert. So if you don't mind we are going to visit a friend in hospital,' said Gran.

'I really am so sorry, Willem. I do hope you will forgive me in time,' said Mrs Hubert, and then she went home.

'But I do want to finish my homework,' I muttered to myself.

We arrived at bed 6 on the Gladstone Ward at 6.12 p.m. There were ribbons and streamers hanging from the curtain round Archie's bed.

'It is not Christmas,' I said.

Archie laughed.

'You'll see,' said Nurse Nancy, winking at me.

Sasha and Fox were walking down the ward towards us.

'STOP,' I said. 'Only 2 visitors allowed.'

'You'll see,' said Nurse Nancy, winking at me again.

'Yeah, wind your neck in, bossy boots,' said Sasha, giving Gran and Archie a kiss.

Fox had the biggest box of chocolates in his hand. I had seen one like it in the window of the Patel's newsagent. It cost £22.50.

'There you go.' Fox handed them round. I had a coffee cream.

I looked up to see Trish, walking down the ward to bed 6.

She hesitated. She looked sad.

'I wasn't sure if I would be welcome,' she said.

Sasha kissed Trish on the cheek.

'Craig left. I chucked him out,' I heard Trish say to my gran. 'Finn and I deserve better. And when Finn has served his time in the secure unit we are going to get on with our lives.'

'This is a new start for you both,' said Gran.

Trish gave her a hug.

'PARTY TIME,' said Nurse Nancy, and 2 medical students walked up to the bed and pulled Archie's blanket back. Underneath, he was fully dressed in his best suit with red socks on. They lifted him out of the bed, being careful of the tube coming out of his arm, and helped him kneel on the floor in front of my gran. He took a small box out of his pocket.

'Gracie,' he said. 'I love you so much. Please would you do me the honour of becoming my wife?'

He took out a ruby engagement ring from the box. 'This was my mother's ring, it made her so happy, and I want it to make you happy.'

'Yes – oh yes,' said Gran, and kneeled down on her old knees opposite him. Tears were pouring down her face. I think they were happy tears.

'Now get up, you old fool,' said Gran, standing up and nodding to the 2 medical students, who lifted Archie back into bed.

Sasha was dancing around laughing, and everyone whooped and cheered. The men in beds 1–5 clapped with us. I shook Archie's hand. Then I spread my arm wings and ran down the ward. I nearly crashed into Nurse Nancy as she wheeled in a trolley of sandwiches. 'CONGRATULATIONS,' she shouted.

I sat on the edge of the bed and had another coffee cream.

I had a grandad.

25

Sasha

I met Willem in the courtyard to read this letter in private.

Dear Sasha and Willem,
    I hope you are both doing allrite. I am doing allrite.
My key worker Bev says I got to address my ~~behavur~~
behaviour, so I am writing to tell you both sorry.
It was ~~cruff~~ cruel and dangerous what I did to you Willem.
I think you are brave. You are braver than me and you
better believe me when I say that is hard to admit.
I am really cut up, Sasha, that you got caught up in all this
and had to see Willem flying and his wings getting broken.
I know that Willem will have told you about my dad.

I think you probably guessed what was going on anyway.
When I first got here I slept and slept till I couldn't sleep
no more. It was good to have my own safe room and to be
away from the Beckham Boyz wanting this and that
from me.

I ~~Cud~~ could sleep sound in my bed knowing that my Dad
would not cum in. Mum says when I am out of here it's going
to be just me and her and Buster of course.

Sasha, thanks for looking after Buster — Mum says
she apresiates it so she can get our flat painted
without interruptions.

I hope he is behaving (fat chance!!!).
Most of the kids here are allrite except for this boy
called Charlie who, as you would say Sasha, is proper
annoying. I still have to do maths and English and stuff.
In group time we had to say 3 things that we was proud of.
Two little things and a big thing.
My number 1 was looking after my pet rat Spud in juniors.
My number 2 was teaching Buster his dog dance
My big number 3 was being part of the Spitfire Club.
Coz I have never been so proud of anything in all my days.
There I've said it.

Mum sent the photos from our presentation and I showed
them to the group.

And guess what? Bev arranged for Donald, an old man what actually flew spitfires, to come and talk to the group. He shook my hand and said he was proud to know me.

I am helping a boy called Merv who is in here. HE is a bit like you Willem, dead clever but finds it hard to make friends. He wants to be a deep sea diver and knows the name of all the fishes whats in the sea. Merv does not like being here with strangers and wearing the ~~gray~~ grey tracksuit that we wear for exercise.

This week I have even won privilege points for
: Cleaning out the fridge.
Digging up the garden
Being a helpful person
This means I can stay up late and have my music to listen to.

Something is kicking off outside. I better see what is happening...

I have just lost privilege points for kicking off at Charlie. Even though I was only trying to stick up for merv.
They have put me in my room for 'time out to reflect on my behaviour'. That is why I am lying on my bed finishing this letter to you. I am looking at photos on the wall of Buster and all of us with Archie standing on Maisy's wing cheering.

Sometimes I wake in the night and reach out for Buster but of course there is nothing there. The emptiness is hard IT makes my bones ach and all the sound of banging doors when I am trying to sleep aggravates me. But I do not kick off.

Well, my arm is aching now after all this writing. I have reflected on my behaviour enuff so I am going to music workshop. I think I would like to learn the electric quitar. I think I would be very good at it.

Luv from Finn

P.S. Please give lots of pats to Buster from me. I miss him.

I folded up Finn's letter.

'Are you sad, Sasha?' Willem asked.

I nodded.

We walked past Archie's garage project.

The sign plastered on the above it said:

Closed due to illness.

It was like the estate was sick too, without Archie's magic. There was just this edginess in the air.

We passed a boy on the street corner who kicked a wall. Willem's hand shook as his boot banged against the wall.

'Cross the road,' said Willem. 'Gran said I must stay away from trouble.'

I had the proper munchies so we went into Bernie's Burger Bar. I ordered a double cheeseburger and chips. Willem had his usual meal number 2. Bernie automatically put his chips and chicken wings in separate boxes.

'Hope Archie comes home soon,' he said. 'He's a bloke in a million. A diamond. There you go.' He put extra chips in our boxes. 'Have those on me.'

'Thank you, Bernie,' we chorused.

A can smashed against the window, clattering as it hit the pavement.

'Oi,' I said, running to the door. Two T Crew boys ran down the road, laughing.

My skin started to prickle. As Willem and I walked back, more and more T Crew and Beckham Street Boyz appeared in the doorways, like scabs on a body:

itchy, sore and angry. It was like the Beckham Estate was getting a fever. Archie's magic was vanishing.

'Let's go see how they're getting on painting Trish's flat,' I said.

We held our breaths in the stinking lift. The stupid thing ground to a halt on the second floor and wouldn't budge, so we walked up the stairs, climbing over boys sitting on the steps who had blocked our path.

'Scuse.' I grabbed Willem's hand and wove a path through them and their sneers, giving attitude as we stepped over them. TJ and Laurence weren't there to watch our backs – they are idiots, but they're my idiots, if you know what I mean. I didn't even know most of these boys.

One I did know, Nathan, with gold teeth, was spraying on a wall:

As we hurried past, Willem pulled out his Spitfire from his pocket and held on to it proper tight until his knuckles went white.

I could hear the sound of Dad playing the old Zebra

Blue track 'Go Go Go' on his guitar, vibrating through the air from our flat.

'Come in,' shouted Trish from the kitchen.

'We've come to help,' I said.

'You're stars,' said Trish.

It was so lovely to see her smiling. She looked really pretty.

'Come on then, give us a hand,' she said, opening another tin of paint and handing us brushes.

And we all painted the kitchen a lovely light blue, like the sky. Dad started playing 'Lizzy Sapphire' and we all started singing along at the tops of our voices.

'*My Lizzy Sapphire sparkling red red red . . .*' Then the guitar stopped and I heard Dad yell, 'BUSTER, COME BACK NOW.'

With a bark, Buster hurtled himself through the front door, into the kitchen, knocked the can of paint over, then ran round in circles printing blue pawprints everywhere. There was a silence while we surveyed the chaos, then we all started to laugh proper hysterically.

Dad put his head round the door.

'Sorry, Buster got out before I could stop him. Right, guys. Let's go to work clearing up this mess.'

'Fox, you are meant to comb your hair before you go to work.'

'WILLEM,' I said, but Dad just laughed.

'Maybe for a special occasion,' he said and he winked at Willem.

We had a lovely afternoon painting and singing, and we gave Buster a bath and we all got wetter than he did.

It was one of those afternoons that stamps itself on your memory.

We were singing the Zebra Blue song 'Angel Missy' when we heard a 'Hello' at the door.

It was Gracie.

'Come in,' shouted Trish.

'Archie's turned the corner,' she said, a tear pouring down her cheek.

Willem ran out of the front door.

'WILLEM,' shouted Gracie. 'Oh, I should have thought before I opened my big mouth.'

'It's all right, Gracie, I'll get him,' I said.

Willem was staring at the corner of the courtyard, waiting for Archie.

'Willem,' I said, 'your gran doesn't mean Archie's going to literally walk round the corner.'

'Oh, where is he?' said Willem, and his proper confused expression cut my heart.

'It means he's getting better, that's what "turned a corner" means.' I held my hand out to Willem and we went back inside where Gracie was saying, 'I said I'll marry him once he can walk me down the aisle.'

We danced and sang and splashed paint on the walls in celebration. Buster barked and did a mad dance on his hind legs. It was like having a family. We were a family.

26

WILLEM

There was a tap, tap, tap, on my window. I opened my eyes.

'Willem, wake up. It's me, Sasha. Get up.'

I heard Buster's whine.

I sat up in bed.

'Willem,' hissed Sasha.

I looked at my alarm clock. It was precisely 5.30 a.m. Today was the day that Archie Thomas Dobbs was coming home from hospital, to his fiancée Gracie May Smith's flat on the 18th floor, Flat 103 of the Beckham Estate, Beckham Street, North West London.

Gran says it is more convenient, as she cannot look after Archie in his flat with all that war paraphernalia cluttering up the place.

I think she wants to help Archie practise walking, so that he can walk her up the aisle and they can get married.

For 2 weeks, Sasha and I have been preparing for this event.

We've been cleaning Maisy and the cars from the garage project every day after school. I also tidied Archie's garage and Maisy's hangar.

'Willem, wake up.'

I went to the window and opened it a tiny bit.

'Sasha, it is not time to get up yet. It is still sleeping time. Go away.'

I went to go back to bed but then Sasha whispered, 'Scramble!'

I had no choice but to obey the Spitfire Club's code word for an urgent and private conversation.

'Get up, Willem, it's lovely out. We're going up to Parliament Hill to pick flowers and put them all over your flat for when Archie comes home. And we can decorate Maisy with garlands. Come on, Willem, it will be a proper surprise.'

I like giving surprises to other people, so I quickly dressed and creeped out of the flat.

* * *

Buster nuzzled my hand to say hello.

We ran through the early morning sunshine, with Buster running round us jumping and barking, and we climbed to the top of Parliament Hill.

We whirled around, looking down at the miniature St Paul's Cathedral and London Eye.

We lay on the grass and spread out our arms and looked at the sky.

Then we picked wild poppies and foxgloves to decorate Maisy and to fill my flat with flowers for Archie.

'Time to go,' said Sasha and we walked back over the Heath through the trees, towards the Beckham Estate. A gentle warm shower started to fall. Buster got excited and ran ahead of us. He started to bark then disappeared behind an oak tree. The leaves on the trees shivered. Sasha and I put out our tongues to catch the raindrops. The branches rustled as the rain fell. Then from behind an oak tree stepped Finn.

Sasha's cheeks went red and she looked down. Buster barked and jumped up at Finn. He kneeled on the grass with his arms round Buster, kissing the top of his head.

The leaves rustled louder. The rain stopped.

Finn was a surprise. I do not like surprises. No words came. My heartbeat became irregular. Finn stood up. I made eye contact like Mrs Hubert said you should do when you want to make friends.

'Finn,' I said, 'have you escaped?'

'No,' he laughed, though I was not making a joke.

Finn rolled up the right leg of his jeans. He had an electronic tag around his ankle. This is a tracking device so the police know where Finn is.

'Been to youth court. Judge gave me a Youth Rehabilitation Order,' said Finn.

Then there was what Gran calls an *atmosphere* in the air. Finn was looking at Sasha. Sasha was looking at Finn. No words came.

Then Finn smiled at her. 'All right, Sasha?'

'All right, Finn,' she said, and flicked her long black hair behind her ears, shook her gold hoop earrings and smiled.

I think they are friends again, but now it is Sasha who is in charge.

And we, the Spitfire Club, walked over the wasteland.

But as we walked towards the courtyard, shouting and banging sounds hit us. We ran faster. The *Closed due to illness* sign had been ripped off Archie's garage and the fence protecting the garage project had been kicked down.

Tools were everywhere and oil was spilled. Our polished cars were ruined.

'Oh no, no – Archie's coming home today,' gasped Sasha.

I kneeled on the floor next to a toolkit turned upside down on the oily floor. I reached for the screwdrivers so I could put them in order. I must make order.

'Who did this?' Sasha shouted, somewhere in the distance.

'We better check on Maisy!' Finn yelled and started running across the courtyard towards the wasteland. Sasha grabbed hold of my hand and dragged me after him towards our Spitfire Club House.

Someone had forced the lock and Maisy's hangar door was open.

And there, in our Club House, were the Beckham Street Boyz and the T Crew – fighting.

Sasha, Finn, Buster and I ran and stood in front of Maisy, protecting our Spitfire.

My world started to melt, but I would not let it. My hands started to jiggle, but I forced them still. I saw the megaphone I had used in the clean-up lying in a ditch by a puddle. I ran to pick it up and climbed on Maisy's wing and shouted through the megaphone in my loudest voice.

'STOP NOW!' I said. 'STOOOOOOOOOOP, PLEASE.' There was what my gran would call *a shocked silence*. Some people had their hands over their ears.

'Archie used his life savings to buy cars for you. Archie respected you. You should respect him,' I said.

'If any of you touch Maisy, you're dead,' said Finn, climbing up next to me. 'Men risked their lives flying her.'

'And women,' said Sasha, stepping up next to Finn.

'The old man's coming home this evening. Are you going to smash up his life? Well, are you? He has done everything for you. Changed your lives,' said Finn.

'He's magic, is Archie,' said Sasha. 'How could you do this?'

The silence crackled.

Then Richie Lane stepped out of the crowd and climbed up on to Maisy, next to Finn and said, 'We'll sort this place. We'll do it for Archie.' He held out his fist and Finn bumped it with his.

In the distance I could see 3 vans driving on to the courtyard of the Beckham Estate and men climbing out of them.

'Perfect timing,' said Finn, waving. 'Those are the supervisors for the Youth Rehabilitation Order. We gotta do graffiti cleaning. We'll get the Beckham Estate shipshape for Archie.'

'Come on, everyone to work,' shouted Sasha.

We, the Spitfire Club, and the boys from the T Crew and Beckham Street Boyz walked back over the wasteland to the Beckham Estate to begin work.

Finn ran ahead to talk to the men in charge of the graffiti cleaning project. I recognized the faces of a lot of the boys who had been on the roof to watch me fly. Laurence was leaning against the van with his hands in his pockets. I smiled at him, but he did not make eye contact with me. The supervisors were organizing the boys into pairs and setting them to work cleaning off TCrew and Beckham Boyz tags from the wall with a special graffiti-removing spray – then scrubbing the wall clean afterwards. Then Aunty Lou marched TJ out of the lift and over to a supervisor with ginger hair who was called Jake. She introduced herself to him. I heard her tell the supervisor to make TJ work hard. I waved at TJ; he gave me a quick smile back.

The remaining Spitfire Club, together with the rest of the Beckham Street Boyz and T Crew, cleaned and tidied the garage. I was in charge of putting the tools back in order. We polished the cars till they gleamed.

Sasha made poppy and foxglove garlands for Maisy. I told her she must not get them near the engine.

And by 6 o'clock the cars were polished and the walls were graffiti free.

An ambulance drove on to the courtyard and down a ramp came Archie in a wheelchair.

I wheeled him over the bumpy grass to see Maisy and crowds of boys followed us. Archie reached out and touched Maisy. He did not speak.

Then I wheeled him to the garage to see the gleaming cars. His eyes twinkled and he clapped his hands and chortled. I think Archie is very happy.

We took him up in the lift to see his fiancée, my gran Gracie.

Sasha pulled me back out on to the balcony and shut my front door.

'Give them some private time,' whispered Sasha.

Then we stretched out our arm wings and ran along the balcony of the 18th floor, laughing.

'Magic man Archie is back. Our estate is no longer sick,' shouted Sasha to the sky.

27

WILLEM

Now that Archie is living with Gran, he lives on the 18th floor, higher than the birds. He says he prefers it up here. He is nearer the sky.

I am calling him 'Grandad' to practise for when they are married.

Sometimes my hands jiggle because things have changed and I do not like change. Archie's possessions are now in our flat. I have tidied them for him. Sometimes he cannot find things and I have to show him where I have put them.

Gran says, 'Willem, you must not touch other people's things.'

'It is not other people. It is Archie,' I tell her.

Archie does what my Gran calls *pottering round* the flat – a little every day, till his legs are strong enough to walk her down the aisle.

Sometimes on a good day, we take Archie for a gentle stroll outside. Our estate is tidier now that the Beckham Street Boyz and T Crew graffiti has been scrubbed off the walls by the boys serving their Youth Rehabilitation Order.

They are still doing all sorts of jobs round the estate. And today I could hear them from inside my bedroom. I was sitting on my bed, spinning the propeller of my model Spitfire Mark 1 to help me concentrate because TJ and Finn were picking up litter by the lift – Jake was supervising them and they were all making a lot of noise.

I could also hear Archie clanging pans as he cooked tea in the kitchen. There were too many bad sounds. Gran was shopping with Sasha and Aunty Lou. I do not like shopping. I hoped she would be home in time for tea.

I spun the propeller of my model Spitfire faster and faster and started working through this aeronautical formula in my head:

$$N_j = \frac{m\,(V_j - V_o)\,V_o}{\frac{1}{2}m\,(V_j - V_o)(V_j + V_o)} = 2\,/\,(1 + V_o/V_j)$$

'Willem, I am making spaghetti bolognaise, would you like some?' Archie called from the kitchen.

'Yes, please, Grandad,' I shouted, 'but—'

'Put the spaghetti and bolognaise on separate plates!' he shouted back, and he laughed though it was not a joke.

I looked at the chart I had made on the wall to show how many days Archie has lived with us and marked off Day 21 with my red gel pen.

'Grandad,' I called from my bedroom, 'do you know how long you have been living with us for?'

But he did not reply.

'Grandad,' I shouted, but there was still no reply.

I ran into the kitchen. The bolognaise was burning, bubbling over the top of the pan.

Archie was on the floor.

'Please get up off the floor, Grandad,' I said. He did not reply. 'Archie?' I said again. His lips were blue. I ran to open the front door and shouted towards the lift.

'Help,' I cried. 'Help me, please – it is Archie.'

Finn, TJ and Jake came running in.

Finn dialled an ambulance from his mobile.

Jake turned off the bolognaise and put the pan in the sink. TJ phoned Aunty Lou so she could tell my gran. He then moved the kitchen table to make more room before kneeling down next to Archie. Our kitchen was very crowded. My hands jiggled. I wanted to help.

'GRANDAD, PLEASE WAKE UP, WE HAVE COME TO ASSIST YOU,' I said in my loudest voice. I do not think Archie heard.

Finn kneeled down on Archie's other side.

Jake made me sit on the chair in the corner, but I wanted to help.

'Archie, please wake up,' said TJ. 'Wake up, please. I let you down. No more stupidness, I promise you. I'm going to become a mechanic, I vow to you on my word. Archie, please wake up . . .' A tear ran down TJ's face.

Archie opened his eyes and his breathing was noisy. Finn held Archie's hand.

'It's me, Finn. Do you forgive me?'

I saw Archie give Finn's hand a little squeeze.

Archie whispered, 'My work here is done.'

He shut his eyes and his face convulsed.

'Out of the way,' said Jake. He put one hand on top of the other on Archie's chest and pressed down as he counted. '1, 2, 3, 4 . . . 1, 2, 3, 4 . . . 1, 2, 3, 4 . . . 1, 2, 3, 4 . . . 1, 2, 3, 4 . . . 1, 2, 3, 4 . . . 1, 2, 3, 4 . . . 1, 2, 3, 4 . . .'

I helped and counted with him.

'1, 2, 3, 4 . . . 1, 2, 3, 4 . . . 1, 2, 3, 4 . . . 1, 2, 3, 4 . . . 1, 2, 3, 4 . . . 1, 2, 3, 4 . . . 1, 2, 3, 4 . . .'

A siren approached the Beckham Estate.

'They're here,' said Finn, and ran out to direct the paramedics to the 18th floor.

'Come on, Archie, breathe. Come on, breathe,' said TJ, and started counting with us. '1, 2, 3, 4 . . . 1, 2, 3, 4 . . .'

The paramedics arrived. A lady in a green jumper took over from Jake pressing on Archie's chest. 1, 2, 3, 4 . . . 1, 2, 3, 4 . . . They opened his shirt and stuck pads on him.

'All of you kids outside now,' said the paramedic man and he cleared us on to the balcony and shut the door – but we could see through the window.

'Stand back,' he shouted and they shocked Archie with an electric current. 1, 2, 3, 4 . . . 1, 2,

3, 4 . . . 1, 2, 3, 4 . . . 1, 2, 3, 4 . . . The lady carried on pressing on his chest.

'Stand back,' shouted the man in the green jumper and they shocked Archie again with the electric current. 1, 2, 3, 4 . . . 1, 2, 3, 4 . . . 1, 2, 3, 4 . . . 1, 2, 3, 4 . . . 1, 2, 3, 4 . . . 1, 2, 3, 4 . . . 1, 2, 3, 4 . . . 1, 2, 3, 4 . . . The lady carried on pressing on his chest.

Gran, Aunty Lou and Sasha got out of the lift and ran towards us.

As Gran pushed open the front door and ran into the kitchen, Aunty Lou grabbed Sasha to stop her following.

'Stand back!' shouted the paramedic and they shocked Archie again. The paramedics pressed on Archie's chest. 1, 2, 3, 4 . . . 1, 2, 3, 4 . . . 1, 2, 3, 4 . . . 1, 2, 3, 4 . . . 1, 2, 3, 4 . . . 1, 2, 3, 4 . . . 1, 2, 3, 4 . . . 1, 2, 3, 4 . . . 1, 2, 3, 4 . . . 1, 2, 3, 4 . . .

It did not work.

Archie died at 17 hundred hours. Everything went into slow motion as we walked towards the kitchen. Gran was kneeling on the floor next to Archie.

'My old man,' she said. 'My lovely magic old

man,' and my gran started to cry.

Sasha put her arms around me and we rocked and sobbed together. Our worlds had melted.

28

Sasha

The four beautiful black horses that pulled Archie's coffin bowed their heads and shook their black plumes as they trotted into the courtyard of the Beckham Estate.

As I looked up, front door after front door opened. Every balcony was filled with people come to pay their respects.

As the clattering of the horses came to a standstill, Gracie stepped forward, holding on to Willem's arm. She placed a Spitfire made of poppies on top of the coffin, then blew the coffin a kiss.

'You are in the sky now, Grandad,' said Willem.

I was wearing the red dress. Gracie had asked me to. 'It's what Archie would have wanted,' she said. She handed me Rachel's handbag with the powder compact inside and Rachel's notes, and squeezed my hand.

'For you, Sasha,' she said.

I couldn't speak. Then Finn put his arm around me and we placed our wreath next to the Spitfire wreath; it simply said, *Magic Man*, made from white flowers.

The cars from the garage project stood in a line; their horns beeped three times in respect. Maisy stood in the middle of the courtyard, a wreath of late summer poppies round her propeller.

Finn helped Gracie into the first car. Aunty Lou, Dad, Trish and TJ were in the car waiting.

The Spitfire Club walked behind the coffin as the procession set off, with me in the middle, holding Finn and Willem's hands.

We made our way slowly, slowly through the streets to St Bartholomew's church. Archie and Gracie had lived together for their twenty-one days of happiness. Exactly the same number of days as Rachel and Robert had spent together in World War Two. I shivered.

Behind the Spitfire Club walked all the Beckham Street Boyz and the Tarkey Crew.

The cars from the garage project, driven by the

elder members followed in a procession behind.

The Fast & Smart sports shop, Bernie's Burger Bar and the Patels' newsagent were closed out of respect. Bernie stood outside with his head bowed, next to the Patels.

As we passed Tarkey House, the people flocked to line the streets. They sprinkled the road with rose petals.

We arrived at the church. It was packed. It felt like my legs wouldn't hold me. Dad was there already; he had combed his hair for Willem and was tuning up his guitar. Gracie had asked me to sing 'Maisy's Rain' as the coffin was carried to its place at the front.

Just before I took my place behind the coffin, a monument on the wall caught my eye. It said:

They laid down their lives for their country.

Then a long list of names carved in stone. My eyes flicked to: *Lt. James Lawson*, *Fredrick Lawson* and, at the end, *Robert Lawson*.

It was him – Rachel's sweetheart. He must have lived around here. They must be brothers. All three of them had died in the war.

I shut my eyes and said a quick prayer for Robert and Rachel. I thanked Rachel for giving me the strength to be free.

A poppy fluttered in the breeze from the top of Archie's coffin. I bent down and placed it on the monument to Robert and his brothers and all the other young men from NW3 who had lost their lives.

I took a deep breath and nodded to Dad. The guitar chords echoed hauntingly round the chapel.

I started to sing 'Maisy's Rain' but my voice shook. Aunty Lou stepped out of her place in the packed congregation and held my hand tight. We walked behind the coffin, singing in harmony.

Then the hymns and prayers and the words from the vicar, Reverend John, all became a blur.

The Spitfire Club walked up to the front with Gracie. Willem and I each held Gracie's hand as the red curtain drew round Archie and, as we said goodbye, each of the Spitfire Club had special words to say; quotes from famous people that we had learned off the internet.

It was my turn first. I said, trying hard to stop my voice wobbling, *'If you were born without wings, do nothing to prevent them from growing.'* Which was words from Coco Chanel, a dress designer.

Then it was Finn's turn. *'The moment you doubt whether you can fly, you cease forever to be able to do it.'* They were the words he said in our Spitfire presentation, from J. M. Barrie, the man who wrote *Peter Pan*. Dad used to read that book to me all the time when I was little.

Willem said a quote from Leonardo da Vinci, the painter and inventor that had designed the wings Willem had built.

'Once you have tasted flight, you will forever walk the earth with your eyes turned skyward, for there you have been and there you will always long to return.'

Willem reached out his hand to touch the coffin. 'Goodbye, Grandad,' he said.

'Goodbye, old man,' said Gracie as the curtain came round and magic man Archie vanished.

I couldn't take no more. I RAN, RAN, RAN out of the church and down the road to the Heath. I could hear Finn and Willem RUNNING behind me, calling me to STOP – but it was like my legs had wings.

The Spitfire Club sat on the top of Parliament Hill and we cried.

I turned and ran and picked wild poppies and

placed them on the spot where Archie had flown the model plane.

I put poppies on the spot where Archie had helped me when I had hysterics after trying to help Willem.

We held hands and danced and whirled around, looking at the miniature London Eye and St Paul's, and our tears became laughter as we remembered the good times.

The wind started to blow. I took the notes out of the black handbag.

'These should be with Rachel,' I said. 'They are not mine to keep. Robert wrote them for his sweetheart Rachel to find.'

I read each one out loud.

An X FOR YOU TO KEEP SAFE UNTIL I COME HOME.
Robert

Rachel, my angel of the sky, will you marry me?

I kissed the paper and held out my hand. The notes flew up, up, up into the sky to Rachel.

I imagined her reaching down for them as they fluttered up, up, past the clouds. 'Thank you, Rachel,' I cried towards the sky.

'We need to get back to Gracie,' I said then.

The Spitfire Club held hands and ran down the hill, and all the way to the Beckham Estate, to Archie's wake at Aunty Lou's.

And as the breeze blew through me I knew with every breath in my body what we, the Spitfire Club, must do.

29

WILLEM

It was precisely 3 a.m. I washed. I dressed.

I tore a page from the back of my Maths exercise book and wrote Gran a note.

18th Floor
Flat 103 Beckham Estate
Beckham Street
Camden Town
London
NW1 7AD

Dear Gran,

Please do not be angry. I do not like it when you are angry.

I know that you are sad. I am sad.

Please forgive me. I know that this is what your fiancé Archie Thomas Dobbs would have wanted.

Your grandson,

Willem Edward Smith

I put the note on the mantelpiece, next to the urn that Archie's burned bones were in. I picked the urn up and put it under my jacket.

I creeped out of the front door and took the lift down to the 11th floor, where Sasha and Finn were waiting. They had their arms round each other. I think they were cold. Buster jumped out of Finn's window and ran along the balcony towards us.

'Buster, you bad dog,' said Finn.

'Let him come,' I said. 'He was Archie's friend too.'

'All right, Willem.' He nodded to me. He picked Buster up in his arms, and Sasha and Finn and I stepped back into the lift.

We went down to our Club House and took in a sharp breath as the door rattled as we opened it.

We did not want to wake up the whole of the Beckham Estate.

I gave Archie's burned bones pot to Sasha to hold.

I felt for the light switch. A cobweb brushed my hand. My fingers jiggled.

Maisy the Spitfire was waiting for us in the dark.

The light went on. We all walked forwards and reached up to touch Maisy's wing. This is how you say hello to an aeroplane.

Then in the doorway stood Richie Lane, Malisha, Tamsin, TJ and Laurence. They helped us push Maisy out of the hangar.

Across the courtyard, out of the nooks and crannies and darkest corner of our estate came boys. Boys that my grandfather, Archie, had turned from rioters into car mechanics. Boys from the Beckham Estate and Tarkey House whom he had turned from enemies into friends.

Some helped us push Maisy. The rest marched behind quietly. Through the dark night we silently pushed Maisy up the road and past the shops.

Up the street we continued silently and on to the Heath.

Then I set to work with my invention that consisted of 2 bags made of canvas and strings.

I fastened the bags to Maisy's wings and climbed into the cockpit and fixed the strings inside.

'We are ready,' I said.

Sasha stepped forward and poured ½ of Archie's burned bones in 1 bag and ½ in the other.

Everyone bowed their heads in respect and then moved back.

I stepped on to the wing and climbed into the cockpit. I was going to achieve my dream. I was going to fly a plane. Sasha and Buster jumped in after me.

Finn stood on the Heath. He didn't move.

'Hurry,' I said. 'Jump in.'

He was shaking.

'I'm scared of flying,' he mumbled, but I heard. So did Sasha.

'GET IN,' she said. 'We're doing this for Archie.'

He didn't move.

I climbed out and stood on the wing. I held out the hand of friendship to him.

'JUMP UP,' I said. 'JUMP.'

Finn jumped.

A note from Sasha

I have never had the jitters so much in all my born days, 'cause let's face it, WILLEM HAD NEVER FLOWN BEFORE – he's only watched Archie and flown in his head.

It was as if magic man Archie had cast his spell one last time 'cause somehow we all fitted into Maisy.

Willem was perched on my lap in the front seat ready to fly, which he assured me was possible and the only way for us all to fit into the Spitfire. Buster and Finn were in the back. We were proper squashed as we were strapped in really tightly with extra safety belts that Willem had designed for the occasion. Finn adjusted the safety belt to fit Buster.

My jitters danced faster, but Willem, he was proper calm and looked back at me and smiled. The engine spluttered, the stink of oil hit my nose and Maisy, three kids and a Staffordshire bull terrier called Buster flew into the dark sky.

It was pure magic. We danced with the clouds and we dipped and swooped.

Then, as the sun rose, I pulled the strings and Archie's ashes fluttered in the breeze and flew into the air – the clouds hugging them, pulling Archie into the sky, where he belonged.

Sasha

EPILOGUE

There was trouble, of course. BIG, BIG, TROUBLE. We ended up on the news and in the papers.

The heading said: **BUSTER AND THE SPITFIRE**.

I don't care though, 'cause it meant now everyone knew about Archie and his magic.

And his magic spread, 'cause garage projects opened on other estates. And I'm not saying it got rid of the gang situation, but it helped.

My dad stopped living in the past, and organized the Archie Dobbs Music Project, in the space under our flats, for the kids on Beckham Estate and Tarkey House. Archie's old piano has pride of place. Trish helped him put up posters and organize the musical instruments. Her face glows with pure happiness these days.

Willem goes sometimes and they are all proper nice to him. He bangs a tambourine to his own rhythm, but that's just fine by everyone.

Dad's teaching Finn the electric guitar. IT'S A PROPER RACKET.

Maisy is the pride of our estate. She stands for what can be achieved when we all pull together.

As for me, I just know that even though I wasn't lucky enough to ever meet Rachel, she did so much for me. Rachel gave me the strength not to run if I don't want to; to run only if I do.

Gracie says it was in me all the time, but knowing Archie and wearing Rachel's dress just brought out in me what had always been there.

I think Buster enjoys his new-found fame from the papers and on the news. He made a special appearance in a reality TV show called *Doggy Stars*. The TV cameras filmed us, the Spitfire Club, sitting in Maisy and walking Buster on the Heath.

The TV camera people were proper nosy. But we never divulged the secret words of the Spitfire Club to them. Our special password 'Maisy's Rain', our special secret code 'scramble', and our special goodbye words 'Chocks away'.

Tamsin and Malisha tried to get in on the action, waving in the background. The producer, Darcy, told them to hop it. HA HA.

The fame's gone to Buster's head. He is even more disobedient, but we all proper love him.

Willem never did win the Headteacher's Cup for Excellence, 'cause of all the trouble we got into. Also Mrs Hubert gave him detention for tearing so many pages out of his Maths book to write notes.

Willem said, 'Some things are more important than winning cups and Maths tests.'

The boy is learning fast!

The Spitfire Club has picnics on the Heath in honour of Archie.

We invite Gracie and Aunty Lou. Sometimes TJ comes and the Patels have been a few times. We have to stop Buster licking the crisps.

The Spitfire Club – Willem, Finn and I – always take a moment to hold hands and look down at the miniature St Paul's and the London Eye, then we look up into the clouds and say goodbye to Rachel and Archie.

Chocks away.

'Once you have tasted flight, you will forever walk
the earth with your eyes turned skyward,
for there you have been, and there you will always
long to return.'

Leonardo da Vinci

Acknowledgements

Thanks to my amazing editor, Naomi Greenwood, who has inspired and nurtured me throughout the journey of *How to Fly With Broken Wings*; Michelle Brackenborough for the gorgeous cover and design; Caitlin Lomas and Lizz Skelly for their never-ending publicity support in these early days of my being an author, and to all at Hodder Children's Books.

To my lovely agent Jodie Hodges and the team at United Agents: Jane, Julian and Emily, thanks for everything.

Peter Thomas for his help with Willem's mathematical genius and to my cousin Sally for her help with the science of light through the glass angel. To Dr Sarah Pottesman for her help with Willem's injury and Andrew Pierce for his Spitfire expertise.

Thank you to Lou Kuenzler and her City Lit workshop where the seeds of *How to Fly* were sown and started to grow and flourish. To the ladies of the Festival Hall for their encouragement (you know who you are!). A special thank you to Vikki Biram and Christopher Ryan for being my first readers and a big thank you to Christopher for taking the photographs at the Dog's Trust and to Marcia for her never-ending belief.

Steve Wilkinson, a big thank you for all your advice and guidance with police matters, and to Paula for coming to my aid with my desperate research. Thanks also to Kavita Birrell for her help. Big thanks to José Bolaño Pinedo for his beautiful fictional architecture plans of the Beckham Estate.

To Ann, Geoff and Paul Neaum and Tracey Smith, Jenny Elson and Clare Calder for their never-ending support.

Curtis Ashton, I could not have done this without your help! Thanks to Helen Buckley and Islington YOT.

Leon Robinson, thank you for guiding me through the joys and history of the Jitterbug and the Jive, and to Julie Robertshaw and Katy Daniels at the Imperial War Museum.

I would also like to thank Aidan and Wendy from the vintage shop Circa who helped me explore the beautiful textures and fabrics of 1940's fashion and for letting me peep in vintage handbags, smell the face powder, feel the silk and embody Rachel's world as she danced the night away in her red dress.

Thanks to Andrew Nelson for his graffiti-removing expertise, Emma Shevah for her help, Sejal Shah for looking over the Patel's dialogue and Charlotte and Simon at the Boma Garden Centre.

To my Aunty Vie for her inspiration and wisdom and my Aunty Barbara and her friends for their support in the bookshops up north!

A big thank you to my Kentish Town City Farm family – the people *and* the animals – for being so lovely. And to Ricardo for sharing with me the story of his precious childhood Staffie, Sasha, who laid the seed of Buster in my imagination.

I would like to pay respect to the extraordinary courage of the young men of World War Two who flew planes in to battle and to mention the men of the ATA who ferried Spitfires and other planes between factories and airfields and to take a moment to remember all those who lost their lives.

How to Fly with Broken Wings *was written to pay homage to those Spitfire Ladies of the ATA, who danced with the clouds as they flew them.*

Bibliography

Flight School by Nick Barnard (Thames & Hudson)

Spitfire Women of World War II by Giles Whittell (Harper Perennial)

Supermarine Spitfire Owners' Workshop Manual by Dr Alfred Price and Paul Blackah (J. H. Haynes & Co. Ltd.)

The Female Few: Spitfire Heroines of the Air Transport Auxiliary by Jacky Hyams (Spellmount Publishers Ltd.)

The following television documentaries were also great sources of information:

Spitfire Sisters (2010) by Fact Not Fiction Films Ltd.

Spitfire women (2011) BBC FOUR

THE STORY BEHIND BUSTER THE STAFFIE

Writing Buster in *How to Fly With Broken Wings* was a joy.
He just jumped off the page and I knew straight away he
had to be a Staffordshire bull terrier.

Staffies are often known as the 'nanny dog' as they are so
good with children and are incredibly loyal, have big hearts
and a sense of fun. I knew Buster the staffie would be the
perfect dog to reach into Willem's world and bring him out
of his shell, and to also bring the best out in Finn. Yet these
beautiful dogs are the most neglected and abused breed
in the country. Our rescue centres are inundated with them.

On the page opposite is a photograph of me with Shireen
from the Dogs Trust, one of the many Staffies that the
Dogs Trust helped find a new home.

Having a dog is a big responsibility but if your family are
looking for a dog please consider rescuing one.

With special thanks to Dogs Trust for allowing me
to meet Shireen!

Founded in 1891, Dogs Trust is the largest dog welfare charity in the UK.
Our mission is to bring about the day when all dogs can enjoy a happy life,
free from the threat of unnecessary destruction. We want to solve the
problem of why there are so many unwanted dogs in the UK and aim to do
this by raising the profile of dogs, promoting dog welfare and encouraging
responsible dog ownership. Each year we care for around 17,000 dogs at
our nationwide network of 19 rehoming centres; no healthy dog is ever
destroyed. For more information please go to www.dogstrust.org.uk